James McCarroll

Nearly a Tragedy

A Comedy in Five Acts

James McCarroll

Nearly a Tragedy
A Comedy in Five Acts

ISBN/EAN: 9783337055028

Printed in Europe, USA, Canada, Australia, Japan

Cover: Foto ©Andreas Hilbeck / pixelio.de

More available books at **www.hansebooks.com**

IN FIVE ACTS.

BY

JAMES McCARROLL.

———

NEW YORK:
JOHN F. TROW & SON,
PRINTERS AND BOOKBINDERS,
209 EAST TWELFTH STREET.
1874.

CHARACTERS.

SIR REGINALD HOWARD, heir to Gray Cliff Manor.

MR. HENRY MORTIMER, a country gentleman in reduced circumstances.

MR. STANHOPE TRAVERS, tutor at the Grange.

MR. EWARD LESTER, sole executor and manager of the Gray Cliff Estates.

DOCTOR HARLEY, physician and old family friend of the Howards.

OLD CAPON, landlord of the White Hart Inn.

MIKE, a confidential Irish servant and man-of-all-work at the White Hart.

TONY LIGHTFOOT, valet to Sir Reginald.

DICK WHITING, servant to the Mortimers.

ALICE, daughter and only child of Mortimer.

LETITIA, a London acquaintance of Sir Reginald.

GYPSY MEG, a wanderer.

SUSAN, maid to Alice.

TENANTRY.

VILLAGERS AND ATTENDANTS.

OFFICERS OF JUSTICE.

NEARLY A TRAGEDY.

ACT I.

SCENE I.—*The White Hart, a country inn near London.* MIKE, *polishing a pewter tankard at the door.* CAPON *and* DICK WHITING *seated in the open air at a table close by, each in the act of finishing a mug of ale.*

DICK. (*Laying down his empty flagon.*) I tell ee what, Master Capon, that there ale is as good as ever was brewed iu Kent ; and I only wish as that young gen'leman as teaches at the Grange yonder could be made to taste a little on't now and then, as it would bring the color to his cheek a bit.

CAPON. (*Placing his empty pot on the table also.*) True, lad, it is good ale ; but when did you ever taste anything else at the White Hart, where I have lived, man and boy, upward of sixty year, and that I have kept for full forty ? And as for Mr. Travers you speak on, I will say he's a proper gen'leman, and a bravish one, too ; for I seed'n myself leap over the wall out of the wood, when Brown Bess was a runnin' away with Miss Alice, and whip the sweet creetur out of the saddle, as if she was ouly a baby, instead of a blessed angel of twenty, as she is.

MIKE. Divil resaive the word of lie in that, Dick ; for I was down there myself jest as she came out of a faiut in his arms. And let me tell you, dear, that bright as that pot is (*holding it out admiringly*), it's ouly a blacky-moor to the blaze of her eyes when she looked up iu his face and began to thank him.

DICK. I know some un as would get his back up at that, Mike, if he heerd on't.

MIKE. (*Contemptuously.*) Sir Riginald ! Is it that miserable craytshure you mane, that, wid all his airs, looks like a hap'orth of soap afther a hard day's washin' ? Be me sowkins, I hope she'll never throw herself away on him, anyway !

CAPON. Yes, Mike, that's all very well ; but you know he has got the Hermitage, and every acre belongin' to it, into his clutches in some way or other !

DICK. Yes, Master Capon, that's where the shoe pinches. Only for it she wouldn't be long makin' short work on him ; but when the roof over one's head is in danger, and there's not much left in the purse, it's hard to work again wealth and power ; although she never gid'n any encouragement, so far as I knows on, and she's my foster-sister.

CAPON. I be main sorry it goes so hard at the Hermitage, Dick ; but what I fear most is, that Sir Reginald doesn't mean fair by the sweet lady.

MIKE. Of coorse he doesn't, and bad luck to him for that same ; but what can you expect from a bewty that tould Misther Lesther, not long ago, that he'd soon be able to put him neck and crop out of the Manor ?

CAPON. And all because he wouldn't break a solemn vow made to Sir Arthur, his father, on his dyin' bed, that he'd never advance him a shillin' over his reg'lar allowance, until he was twenty-five, when he was to come into the estates accordin' to the will ; and that he himself would, married or single, live at the Manor and manage all the property just as if it was his own, until the time had run out.

DICK. Ay, sure, and well he managed it, too ; for it has near doubled in vallee under him ; although he had often to threaten that he'd put this precious customer out of doors. and not let him enter the Manor again until his twenty-fifth birth-day ; which he could do, accordin' to some papers as Sir Arthur signed.

MIKE. Begorra, I wish it was him that died in France long ago, instead of Misthress Mansfield's little son, that you were spakin' of yestherday, Misther Capon.

CAPON. Yes, Mike, Lady Howard, arter the death of Sir Arthur, took this widow to her heart, and when she herself was a dyin', gid her the charge of this Sir Reginald, who was about the age of her own little un, and that she was to bring up accordin' to his rank, so far as his allowance went.

DICK. And a nice bringin' up she gid'n, although she and Sarah Waters had only him to take care on ; for little Fred, as I heerd they called'n, died a month arter he left England.

MIKE. Of coarse ! It's always the bad ones that's left to comfort us.

CAPON. Sartin sure, Mike, I've seed it often. They stayed away until he was ten years old, and then brought'n back to torment us, although Sir Arthur and my Lady were as noble creeturs as ever broke bread.

DICK. Didn't the widow Mansfield soon die arter her return ?

CAPON. Yes. A few weeks arter ; but not afore she got Mr. Lester to make Sarah Waters head-housekeeper, that she has now been at the Manor full fifteen year.

MIKE. But what about Nancy Evans, that you and the docther was talkin' about the other evenin' ?

CAPON. Oh ! ay, Nancy was my Lady's foster-sister, and was a nus-sin' Sir Reginald at the time of her death. The night afore she died she sent for her, and arter gid'n her enough to put her above work all her days, made her take an oath, privately, that, if possible, she'd never lose sight on him till he comed into his property.

DICK. So I've heerd. She thought, arter all, it wasn't wise to leave the care of her only child to one as was no relation, and wanted Nancy, as she knew loved'n, to be about'n till he growed up.

CAPON. Yes, but they took'n from her a day or two arter my Lady was buried. So when he and little Fred was tooked abroad, because they wouldn't let her go with'n, she left the Manor, and has never been heerd on since.

MIKE. Well, by the mortial, if they even did lave her go wid them, she'd have more than a fish to fry to take care of that joker, that's as kantankerous as a mule, and as sour as a gallon of vinegar sharpened down to a pint.

DICK. That he be; for everybody, gentle and simple, hates'n; and besides, it's not long since, as the Lunnon solicitors and Mr. Lester were near gid'n on him a horsewhippin' for what he said about the way they were doin' summat regardin' the estates.

CAPON. He's a bad un, Dick, and has always keeped bad company.

MIKE. Yis! and there's no signs of his improvin'; for I harde, a night or two ago, that that Gipsy Meg, who wandhered into this place lately, is some sort of a divilish spy of his, and tells him everythin' that's said about him, however the ould witch finds it out.

DICK. I heerd summat of that, too, Mike; and know myself that she's to be found prowlin' about the wood at all hours, with that long gray cloak and red handkercher on her head; but the worst on it is, they say she owes a grudge to Master Travers as she's goin' to pay; and if she does, we all know Sir Reginald is at the bottom on it, that hates'n because he has begun a visitin' the Hermitage of late.

MIKE. Spake of the divil an' he'll appear; for there's Sir Riginald himself, tyin' his horse up at the gate. (*Pausing and looking for a moment.*) Yis! here he comes, as full of ould Harry as an egg's full of mate!

Enter SIR REGINALD, *booted and spurred, with a riding whip in his hand.* DICK *and* CAPON *arise as he approaches;* MIKE *resumes his polishing.*

SIR REGINALD. (*Walking up to* DICK, *and giving him a sharp cut of the whip across the shoulders.*) How, now, fellow! What are you doing here this hour of the morning, instead of being at the Hermitage about your master's or mistress's business?

DICK. (*Assuming a menacing attitude.*) No more of that, Sir Reginald, you're not my master or mistress either! No more of that, or I'll——

SIR REGINALD. (*Raising the whip again.*) What, sirrah! Do you threaten? Be off this moment, or I'll trounce you within an inch of your life!

DICK. (*Standing his ground without flinching.*) I'm not so sure of that! Don't strike again, Sir Reginald; for I feel myself gettin' a little bit queerish; and in for a penny, in for a pound, you know!

SIR REGINALD. (*Taken a little aback, and turning to* CAPON.) Put this fellow off the premises, and never let him set foot on them again, on pain of my displeasure. Remember your lease of the White Hart expires in a few days, and I alone have power to renew it!

CAPON. (*Bowing.*) I know, Sir Reginald; but I have a lease of a little bit of property that I think more on than even this dear, old spot, and that would expire this instant, if I was to turn my back on any honest lad at the biddin' of another—I mean the respect that's accorded to these few gray hairs by all as knows me. I'm here to make my bread decently, by gentle and simple, and to maintain the character of a true man; and that I'll do (*extending his hand to* DICK, *who shakes it warmly*) if there's no other roof to shelter this head but the one as now shines above both on us.

MIKE. (*Flourishing the tankard above his head.*) Hurra! Hurreye! Hurroo! Bad luck to the sich a speech did I ever hear since I was in the Four Coorts! Oh! I'd give the world if Miss Alice was here! Wouldn't she give you as sweet a look as she gave Misther Thravers when she came out of that faint in his arms! Dick, come in, avick, till we dhrink his health in a private dhrop that never passed undher the nose of a gauger. [*Exeunt* MIKE *and* DICK.

SIR REGINALD. (*With a fierce and diabolical leer.*) As you please, Master Capon. But of one thing rest assured, your days at the White Hart are numbered!

CAPON. Well, Sir Reginald, that be main hard arter so many years; but I suppose what must be, must! In coorse, it will be sad enough to leave what I almost looked upon as my own. I'll miss the early song of the birds in the wood yonder, and the breath of the hawthorn blossoms in the lane; but it is better that I should lose everything than the self-respect as sings clearer and smells sweeter than 'em all.

SIR REGINALD. That's enough! My resolve is fixed; but what did that fellow of your's mean regarding Miss Mortimer?

CAPON. Not much, Sir Reginald. My brown mare runned away with her t'other day, and might have killed her, only the handsome tutor at the Grange, who happened to be readin' in the wood, leaped out before her, at the risk of his life, and arter throwin' the wild beast completely on her haunches, whipped the sweet lady out of the saddle, as she fainted away in his arms.

SIR REGINALD. (*Aside, scowling deeply*). By heavens! I haven't heard a word of this; although I know that lackey at the Grange has been at the Hermitage of late. Never fear, I shall look after her narrowly, and crush her, never to rise again, if I find she dares to entertain even a friendly feeling for that beggar, who has to depend on Greek and Latin for his breakfast! (*To* CAPON.) Oh! yes, I remember hearing something of it from Miss Mortimer, but she did not seem to set such value on this service as you do. However, I shall speak to her again on the subject, and if this poor devil has been at any trouble I shall see that he is rewarded. In the meantime, Master Capon, you may prepare to bid adieu to the White Hart! [*Exit* SIR REGINALD.

CAPON. (*Pausing on the threshold while entering the inn, and looking round after* SIR REGINALD.) Thank God! I beant worth twenty pound in the world! [*Exit* CAPON.

SCENE II.—*Library in the Hermitage. Enter* MORTIMER *and* TRAVERS, *conversing. They seat themselves near a window opening on the lawn.*

TRAVERS. Yes, dear sir, as you were observing, there is an apparent lack of genius and solid attainments among large numbers of the aristocracy; but I think you might have added, the upper classes of all countries.

MORTIMER. Perhaps so; for the germs of progress and intellectual greatness seem to be thickly and deeply planted only in that wide, mellow furrow that runs between wealth and penury.

TRAVERS. Yes, but this does not, I think, involve necessarily any inherent barrenness of soil on the part of the two extreme classes, the rich and the poor, to whom you allude.

ALICE, *appearing in the open window, or glass doorway.*

ALICE. Ah! Mr. Travers, how do you do? (*Enters the room and extends her hand.*) I was on the lawn near the wood when I saw you ascending the terrace.

TRAVERS. Had I observed you, Miss Mortimer, I should have done myself the pleasure of joining you. (*Rising.*)

ALICE. (*Turning to* MORTIMER.) But have I interrupted you, papa? You were in conversation. (*Takes a chair.* TRAVERS *resumes his seat.*)

MORTIMER. No, my dear. Mr. Travers was merely making some remarks upon the different classes of society.

TRAVERS. I was simply observing, Miss Mortimer, in relation to the upper, the middle, and the lower classes, that there is no inherent mental inferiority or superiority in any one of them beyond another. If the lower classes are not so advanced as the middle, it is because they have time to think with their bone and muscle only; if the middle classes are more exalted, it is because they are able to use their brains and their fingers alternately, which they are constrained to do in some

1*

way ; and if the upper classes do not excel these latter again, it is because they are not constrained to either think or work.

ALICE. A most original and philosophic view of the case, Mr. Travers; and you will, no doubt, say that, under good government, these classes, like the three primal colors in a pencil of white light, may be blended so harmoniously as to be lost in one common radiance.

TRAVERS. Very beautifully expressed, Miss Mortimer ; but I fear the millennium you have illustrated so charmingly is not close at hand.

MORTIMER. And so I fear, too, Mr. Travers. But have you met Sir Reginald Howard since you came among us?

TRAVERS. No. I hear, however, that he is seldom at the Manor.

MORTIMER. Not often. Mr. Lester, who is lord and master there yet, and he have never pulled well together. But some allowance ought to be made in relation to the follies of the heir to such wealth, who has lived so long in London.

ALICE. (*With earnestness.*) Yes, papa; but there is a very great difference between what may properly be termed follies, and deliberate acts of infamy, the offspring of innate depravity.

MORTIMER. Alice, my dear, your observations may mislead Mr. Travers, coming, as they do, so close on my reference to Sir Reginald.

ALICE. I should be sorry to do the slightest injustice to any one, papa !

MORTIMER. (*Changing the conversation.*) You lived in London, I hear, before you came to the Grange, Mr. Travers. Does your family reside there?

TRAVERS. Yes, I was engaged in the city for some time ; but of my family, or even my birthplace, I know nothing whatever.

MORTIMER. (*With surprise.*) Indeed !

ALICE. (*With interest.*) How strange !

TRAVERS. Until recently I supposed I was born on the Continent, the son of a very learned but poor English clergyman who had long resided abroad for the sake of his health ; but who, on the late downfall of Napoleon, returned to this country, where he died soon after, leaving me, as my only heritage, what is said to be a good classical education, and an attested document, handed to me in his last moments, setting forth that, when I was about two years old, he found me in charge of a dying man, a suspicious character, who had met with a fatal accident, and who deposed that, two or three days previously, he had been suborned by some unknown party to make away with me; but that, when he was carrying me off to the wretched hut in which he lay, he had been followed by a woman who seemed to have divined his purpose, and who dissuaded him from committing the crime, agreeing to take me off his hands on the following day, and bear me away where I should never again be heard of. The man breathed his last a few moments after making this declaration ; and as he lived quite alone and seemed utterly destitute, the clergyman, whose name I bear, took me home with him, awaiting the reappearance of the woman. She came, and taking down his name, address, and even the place of his birth, promised to return the next day. He never saw her afterwards, and, as he was childless, I became his son!

ALICE. (*Tenderly.*) Poor child! What an escape! (*Smilingly.*) Well, then, Mr. Travers, you may have some of the bluest blood of the land in your veins for aught you know.

TRAVERS. Ah! Miss Mortimer, my birth and slender purse are, I fear, wedded most lawfully; but this does not trouble me much, for although I am far from despising wealth or station, I think that true nobility may be found outside as well as within their circle.

MORTIMER. (*With generous emotion.*) True! Mr. Travers, wealth and station, without innate worth, have no more true value than the mere gaudy trappings of the stage that so often dazzle us!

ALICE. Bravo, papa! Well and nobly said; but as you have incidentally mentioned the stage, doubtless Mr. Travers, during his residence in town, saw a good deal of it.

MORTIMER. Oh! I see! You are verging towards a favorite topic of yours.

TRAVERS. Yes, Miss Mortimer, I did see something of it, to the removal of some of my prejudices. I had been taught to consider its tendencies injurious, but found the theatre, in even its least exalted aspect, immeasurably in advance of the street or the gin-shop. Where large numbers of even the lowest classes are drawn together promiscuously they are more decorous and subject to greater restraints than if they were scattered through the intemperate and immoral resorts of a town or city in twos and threes, which they should certainly be, were it not for some central point of attraction such as the theatre. Were it not for the stage, there are thousands upon thousands of poor persons to-day that would have no true idea of the costumes, manners, and customs of the past, or of real life in the present day outside the contracted sphere in which they move. Through its heroes and heroines it fosters, as a general thing, noble aspirations, and seldom represents anything half so bad as may be met in books now found in the hands of countless readers. In fact, great as may be the painter and the sculptor, their creations, in an educational point of view, fall far short of those of the drama or stage. With them, all action is fixed in one eternal pose. The Christ of Rubens has not yet descended from the Cross, nor have the marble serpents of "The Laocoon" yet strangled the priest of Apollo and his two sons. In varying language, as in life and action, the living, glowing pictures of the stage transcend all mere works of art. And hence we may properly regard it as an abiding source of intelligence and amusement, in whose shining depths we may, with advantage, lave, at times, the dusty limbs of labor and of thought.

MORTIMER. Really, Mr. Travers, you are a most eloquent advocate of the drama!

ALICE. Yes, papa, and a most just one also!

MORTIMER. And a most generous one, if you will, my dear. But is not that a glorious sunset! (*Pointing through the window.*)

TRAVERS. (*Rising and approaching the open casement.*) It is truly resplendent. Is it not, Miss Mortimer?

ALICE. (*Advancing to* TRAVERS'S *side.*) It is indeed magnificent! On the verge of the horizon, what a fairy-land of crimson and purple and gold! (*With a slight start.*) Oh! here comes Sir Reginald Howard! He is just at the door.

MORTIMER. (*Aside.*) The deuce! Rather awkward! I thought he was in London.

Enter SIR REGINALD, *who, with a deep scowl, on recognizing* ALICE *and* TRAVERS *standing together, halts for a moment in the doorway.*

SIR REGINALD. (*Regaining his composure, advances towards* MISS MORTIMER *with a scarifying leer, and extends his hand.*) How do you do, Miss Mortimer? (*Shakes hands.*) Pray excuse my presence at such an inopportune moment; but the fact is, having just returned from town, I could not deny myself the pleasure of calling at once and paying my respects.

ALICE. (*Quite composedly.*) You are very gracious, Sir Reginald. But as to the moment being inopportune, I regard it quite the reverse, as it affords me the pleasure of introducing Mr. Stanhope Travers. (*Both are introduced, and bow stiffly; on which* SIR REGINALD *turns abruptly away and seats himself beside* MR. MORTIMER, *who seems ill at ease.*)

SIR REGINALD. (*Addressing* MORTIMER *in evident bad humor.*) Before leaving for town, sir, I had no opportunity of apprising you that you have in your service a ruffian called Whiting, who recently threatened, without the slightest provocation, to assault me; and who, during my absence, abused my valet in a most wanton and cruel manner!

ALICE. (*Stepping suddenly forward in anger, and addressing* SIR REGINALD). Dick Whiting, my foster-brother, although a servant and uneducated, is no ruffian, Sir Reginald! He is respected by all who know him, whose respect is worth having. I shall not, now, venture to say whether he was or was not justified in resenting your gratuitous cut of a whip at the White Hart, on the occasion you refer to; but this I will say: had he not punished that valet of yours for attempting to emulate you with his switch, he would have sunk to a very low point in my estimation!

SIR REGINALD. (*With deep mortification and anger.*) Miss Mortimer!

ALICE. Exactly, Sir Reginald! And were I a man, and the poorest and humblest in the land, I should not suffer the whip of the proudest or greatest in it to be laid across my shoulders with impunity; not to speak of the switch of a low, mischief-making lackey, who is not only a reproach to the place, but a disgrace to the livery he wears!

SIR REGINALD. (*Scarcely able to contain himself.*) Thank you, Miss Mortimer! And in the presence of a stranger, too!

TRAVERS. (*Severely.*) Your reference to me, sir, is uncalled for. If Miss Mortimer felt my presence embarrassing in any degree, she would have selected some other period for her remarks.

SIR REGINALD. (*Sharply.*) I did not address you, sir!

TRAVERS. You referred to me, sir, and in my hearing!

MORTIMER. (*In a state of great excitement.*) Gentlemen! gentlemen!

SIR REGINALD. (*Glancing superciliously at* TRAVERS.) What do you mean by "gentlemen!" Mr. Mortimer? I hope you don't regard the term to be without some restriction!

MORTIMER. (*Becomes suddenly aroused at the insult offered to* TRAVERS *beneath his roof, while the latter eyes* SIR REGINALD, *with folded arms.*) This is neither just nor courteous, Sir Reginald! Alice, my dear, you had better withdraw!

ALICE. (*Extending her hand to* TRAVERS, *who takes it.*) Adieu, for the present! Send me some books to-morrow!

[*Exit* ALICE, *with a cold, formal curtsey to* SIR REGINALD.

TRAVERS. (*Stepping close to* SIR REGINALD.) Now that I am unembarrassed by the presence of a lady, although not yet quite free (*glancing at* MORTIMER), let me inform you that, had you been guilty, in any other place, of the wanton insult you have offered me, I should have inflicted the severest personal chastisement on you!

SIR REGINALD. (*Starting to his feet, and addressing* MORTIMER.) Will you, sir, permit me to be insulted in your presence by this person, from whom I cannot obtain or demand the satisfaction due to my rank; although he seems to be on the most intimate terms with both you and your daughter?

TRAVERS. Coward! Coward!

SIR REGINALD. (*Without appearing to notice the interruption.*) This roof is still yours for a short period at least, and you ought to exercise some authority beneath it!

MORTIMER. (*Bounding from his chair in a fury of anger.*) This, Sir Reginald, is more than even I shall suffer at your hands tamely; for you not only refer, in a most heartless manner, to my shattered fortunes, but intimate that I and Miss Mortimer have formed an unworthy acquaintance. As, however, you have feelingly observed that this roof is yet mine for a brief space, I shall take advantage of the circumstance, and wish you a very good evening!

SIR REGINALD. (*Retiring towards the door, with a demoniacal expression of countenance, while* MORTIMER *sinks into a chair.*) So! so! Mr. Mortimer! We shall see whether you are so grandiloquent in a day or two! Pray make my compliments to your amiable daughter. (*Lingering in the doorway*). Won't you, kind sir? (*With a fiendish laugh.*)

TRAVERS. (*Striding towards* SIR REGINALD.) Away! away! lest I
trample you into dust!   [*Exit* SIR REGINALD, *with alacrity.*

MORTIMER. (*Slowly rising from his chair.*) This has been very un-
pleasant for both of us, Mr. Travers. I am quite glad Miss Mortimer with-
drew as soon as she did; although the poor child has been long aware
that the roof that shelters us is sorely embarrassed. Let us step out on
the lawn. (*Taking his arm.*) The cool air will refresh me.

TRAVERS. Calm yourself, dear sir! and take counsel from the pro-
verb, " All is not lost that's in danger! "   [*Exeunt.*

END OF ACT I.

ACT II.

SCENE I.—*A wood extending between the Hermitage and the Grange.*
*   TRAVERS seen walking and reading in the shade.*

TRAVERS. (*Closing his book wearily, and pausing.*)
'Tis all in vain!   For me there's no relief!
These pages, that had once possessed such charms,
Now trail their beauties upon broken wing!
O! how supremely glorious did she look
When, in her humble servitor's just cause,
She struck that paltry dastard to the heart
With the keen shafts of her indignant scorn!
But she returned not with a fond " Good-night! "
And I am but an accidental friend!   (*Sadly.*)
From these desponding doubts, oh! whence escape?
Or where take refuge from those lustrous eyes
That filled the crimson beaker of my heart
With this hot, frenzied flood of luscious wine,
Till at a bound, with my own life-blood drunk,
I madly open flung my bosom's gates,
And bid this bright creation to a feast
Where I myself a skeleton now sit,
Like that grim guest at the Egyptian's board!
Was it for this that I had fought so long
Against hard fortune and my humble birth,

Or trimmed the midnight lamp o'er boastful lore,
That thus deserts me in my sorest need ?
> (*Striking the volume with his clenched hand.*)

Oh ! vain philosophy, where art thou now ?
What of thy frostwork on this window pane—
> (*Placing his hand on his heart.*)

Thy pictures hung upon these naked walls ?
> (*Fluttering his hand over the region of his heart.*)

Dissolved beneath the light of those dark orbs,
And the warm sighs that winged the words of thanks
That struggling from their pris'n of pearl and rose,
In broken music fell upon my ear,
As she a moment lay within these arms !
> (*Extending his arms.*)

But, I am weary of myself and thought,
And here shall rest me in the quiet shade,
And seek a friendly void, however brief,
In which my lab'ring soul may find relief !
> (*Advancing to a rustic seat and sinking listlessly upon it.*)

ALICE *entering the wood close by the Hermitage.* GIPSY MEG *discovered concealing herself in a copse hard by, where she stands listening.*

ALICE. (*Pausing after a few steps, without apprehending the proximity of either* MEG *or* TRAVERS.

What true nobility ! Though poor, how proud !
And with what dignity and polished grace
He met that rude assault of wealth and power,
Though fierce the light that burned within his eyes !
> (*Placing her hand on her heart.*)

Be still ! be still ! Poor fluttering heart, be still !
Nor send so oft this crimson, tell-tale flood
Along the shallows of my cheek and brow
To beat against the iceberg of my brain,
And be thrown back again, chilled through and through !
A few brief days ! Oh ! what a change they've made !
No longer now myself, I only dream
Of the sweet spell that so enthralled my sense
When, by this very wood, now scarce a month,
I woke to consciousness within his arms,
That just had snatched me from the jaws of death !
I loved him from that moment ! 'Twas my fate !
Although his breast may make a cold return,
For I have heard great learning chills the blood !
But I this trembling secret can disguise,
So that it shall escape all ears and eyes ! (*Continues to walk.*)

MEG. (*Emerging from her concealment and standing before her.*) May it please you, sweet lady, cross my palm with silver, and you shall know the future and the past from my lips. (*Extending her hand.*)

ALICE. (*Smilingly.*) Good mother, I am sore afraid that, if you divine truly, there is sad news in store for me and mine. But take this piece of silver, and read the tangled lines of this hand, if you will. (*Extending both hand and silver.*)

> I shall not shrink from what they may reveal,
> For I have felt near all that I can feel!

MEG. (*Taking her hand and scrutinizing it closely.*) What do I here behold! Two rivals in deadly conflict! The one penniless and learned; the other rich and haughty! And here steals into view a beautiful young creature, full of love and goodness,

> Who on the humbler turns a sweet, bright face;
> Though birth and fortune yet shall win the race!

ALICE. (*Suddenly withdrawing her hand.*)

> Enough! Good gypsy mother, I must go;
> No more of this wild romaunt would I know!

MEG. (*Looking Alice earnestly in the face.*) Wild romaunt! Tell me, who stood by yonder copse on yestermorn with a bruised wild, flower in her hand, and cried, "How like my heart this is," and sighed, and sighed, and sighed again the name of that poor rival? And who was it that, but scarce a minute since, within this very wood, confessed to herself, half aloud, that she loved him since the moment he first snatched her from the jaws of death?

ALICE. (*In great trepidation and alarm.*) Great heaven! I am undone! Oh! good gypsy mother! Oh! kind gypsy mother! Take pity upon me! Have mercy upon me!

> And this my secret keep at any cost;
> For if you once reveal it, I am lost!

MEG. Your secret's safe enough, Alice Mortimer! I remember your mother!

> But now I must away to some lone dell,
> In search of herbs to work a potent spell!

(*Disappears among the trees.*)

ALICE. (*With great emotion, and while gazing, as if fascinated, after* MEG.) How terrible! And I have been my own executioner!

[TRAVERS *now discovers her standing in the distance, and at once approaching, reaches her as she, without perceiving him, is about to retrace her steps to the Hermitage.*]

TRAVERS. (*While* ALICE *starts at the sound of his voice.*) More wildflowers in the wood! Sweet lady—Miss Mortimer, I mean—I am glad to perceive that the annoyances of last evening have not preyed upon your cheek.

ALICE. Oh! Mr. Travers, you startled me! I thought I was

quite alone. (*Extending her hand.*) Did you see that gypsy-woman who has just left me? She has been quite unnerving me with her strange predictions and knowledge of things.

TRAVERS. I have not seen her to-day, although she may have seen me; for she is almost always to be found in some part of the wood, near the Hermitage or the Grange.

ALICE. She is a singular creature, and I fear no friend of yours. At least I infer so from a remark she made.

TRAVERS. Indeed! Well, I must console myself with the conviction that I am void of all offence against her; although she says she has crossed my path in other lands.

ALICE. That's strange! But they are a singular race, and liable to turn up in the most unexpected places.

TRAVERS. May I hope that Mr. Mortimer is quite well; and that he suffers no ill effects from the excitement of last evening?

ALICE. Why, thank you, he is quite well, and is loud in his praise of the manner in which you acquitted yourself.

TRAVERS. I was sorely tried, Miss Mortimer, I assure you!

ALICE. Yes, papa told me so; and that you had nearly lost all command of yourself when Sir Reginald made some sneering observation relative to me.

TRAVERS. It was at that point I had to impose bands of triple steel upon myself; for where you are concerned, Miss Mortimer, the dread of consequences disappears at once, and life itself is but a feather in the scale! (*With great earnestness.*)

ALICE. (*Embarrassed with intense emotion; but offering her hand, which he carries respectfully to his lips.*) You are good and brave and kind, Mr. Travers; and what can I say more, than that I feel I owe you my life?—a boon I can never repay; and if I can, pray tell me how.

TRAVERS. (*With sudden and startling fervor.*) With your love! with your love! Alice Mortimer! without which all this fair world is a desert to me.

ALICE. (*Softly withdrawing her hand, and trembling violently.*) Oh! Mr. Travers! For Heaven's sake, hush! These trees have ears, as I have just learned to my cost! But now I must return to the Hermitage. Adieu! (*Extending her hand again, which TRAVERS seizes excitedly, presses to his lips, and retains.*)

TRAVERS. Adieu! But ere you leave this spot, if you would spare me many a bitter thought and anguished throb, oh! bid me hope, at least. (*Covering her hand with kisses.*)

ALICE. (*In a state of painful excitement, while releasing her hand softly once more.*) There now; pray let me go; and if you fain would hope, you well may do so; for now I feel I have no heart to carry hence! Adieu! Adieu! (*Tenderly.*)

TRAVERS. Adieu! Beloved, adieu!

[*Exit* ALICE, *kissing her hand to* TRAVERS.

(Solus.)

The chrysalis is broken, and I mount
The bright empyrean upon golden wings!
Oh! what a silver lining to the cloud
That had o'ershadowed me from day to day!
How sweet the birds sing in yon hazel copse;
And what strange fragrance fills the purple air.
All things are beautiful! The earth and sky
Have melted into one broad paradise!
There is nor pain nor sorrow in this world,
But the frail husks of an abounding bliss
That we misname, not knowing their true use!
Oh! how shall I regain my hold on earth,
Or win my spirit back to things of sense?—
But stay! With all this heav'n of light and love,
What if the shattered fortunes of her sire
Consign her to that high-born dastard's arms?
Then would I court some final, fatal stroke! (*Fiercely.*)
Though, swift descending through my maddened brain,
It smeared my lips and filled my quivering throat
With the hot vintage of my cloven skull! (*Turning to leave the wood.*)
But hold! With Fate itself I'll dare to cope;
Her love so fills my soul with strength and hope!   [*Exit* TRAVERS.

Enter TONY LIGHTFOOT, *emerging stealthily from a thicket, close by where*
ALICE *and* TRAVERS *had been standing.*

TONY. (*Peering cautiously about him with a wicked leer.*) Saw it all!
Heard it all! Know it all! Glorious! Hurra! (*Sotto voce.*) Capital!
Tony, you're in luck! Billing and cooing! Vowing eternal love! Fond
adieus! and kissing of hands and fingers! Sir Reginald's at a discount,
Tony! How will he like that? Not well! Tony answers, Not well!
But he may succeed yet, for all that! How, Tony? Fye! Fye! for
asking such silly questions! You know how! Gypsy Meg carries a long
knife, I warrant you! They say she hates this romantic tutor, who is to
be found in the wood almost every evening at dusk, passing either to or
from the Hermitage. A gypsy's purse is always empty! Enough said,
Tony! and no matter if she swings for it after! I know Sir Reginald!
He won't stick at trifles when there's a rival in the way! Tony, you're
in luck! Would you like to keep the White Heart? Yes! You have
a taste for innkeeping. But you must be cautious, and get that dear,
devilish hyena of a master of yours as deep in the mud as you're in the
mire! He is a magistrate, will now have wealth untold at his command,
and can, therefore, stand between you and danger! Take him into your
confidence, Tony! He likes you because you're a gentleman's gentleman

of the first water! Go, then, and get up that ugly back of his! Make him show his sharp, white teeth! Tell him what you have heard and seen! Make him snap his fierce lantern jaws like a wolf! Handle the ropes carefully and you're all right! Go to him and turn his thin lips blue, and his small eyes green! Tony, you're in luck! Now for a bold stroke, and your fortune's made.   [*Exit* TONY.

Re-enter MEG, *creeping from some underwood that had been almost beneath* TONY'S *feet.*

MEG. (*Rising slowly and looking cautiously about her.*) So! so! Master Tony! You have it all your own way! Well, whatever settlement I may have to make with this rival you speak of, will be made in my own way and on his own account solely! Leave him to me, Master Tony! I can manage him a great deal better than either you or " that dear, devilish hyena of a master of yours," as you call him; although, should I silence him, quietly, in the interests of Sir Reginald, you were considerate enough to say that it was no matter if I swung for it afterwards! That was ungenerous! Well, the plot thickens, and I must away, Tony:

> For if you now have found so much to do,
> 'Tis strange if I can't find a little too.

[*Exit* MEG.

SCENE II.—*Apartment in the Manor. Enter* LESTER, *alone, poring over some papers.*

LESTER. (*Wearily.*) Thank heaven, I shall soon be rid of this painful trust. I was his father's bosom friend, and knew his mother well. They were a noble pair! Then, how he came to turn out a wretch so vile, I can't divine; but so it is! We part, as we have been for years—enemies!—and all because I would not break that solemn vow, and pander to his vicious heart and brain. Well, I am consoled by the reflection that, through all this lapse of time, free from the cares of a married life, I have done faithfully by his interests and my own good name. (*Sinks into a chair ; hears a rap at the door*). Come in!

Enter DOCTOR HARLEY.

DOCTOR. (*Briskly.*) Good-morning, Lester! How do you do?
LESTER. (*Rising. They shake hands.*) Doctor, I am glad to see you! Take a chair. (*Resumes his seat.*)
DOCT. I can't stay just now; I merely called to see Waters, that housekeeper of yours, who, when I was prescribing for her yesterday, said she had something of a private and very serious character to lay before me as a magistrate.
LESTER. Indeed! Although I have seen that woman almost daily for

the last fifteen years, I never could make her out thoroughly; and have been always of the opinion that her mind is not at ease.

DOCT. Now that I recollect, people do say she is in the habit of talking to herself, like that gypsy Meg, whom, by the way, I have just passed in the hall. I heard her tell one of the servants that she wanted to speak to you.

LESTER. What can she have to say to me?

DOCT. That I am unable to tell you. But good-by for the present; I may see you again after I hear what Waters has to say. Shall I send that gypsy in as I pass her?

LESTER. Yes, thank you. Be good enough to leave the door open, and bid her enter without any ceremony.   [*Exit* DOCTOR.

Enter MEG.

MEG. Good-morning, Mr. Lester, if it's not too late; for I don't see the cuckoo clock standing in the corner there (*pointing*), that told the hours so pleasantly when you and Sir Arthur used to ride over to the Oakes to see the woodmen at work, now many a long year ago.

LESTER. (*Looking narrowly at her.*) In truth, good dame, you awaken somewhat sad recollections at this peculiar time. But how a stranger, like you, come to know aught of this, for the clock has long since disappeared from that nook, I am at a loss to say.

MEG. (*Without seeming to notice this observation.*) And there's good Doctor Harley, who just passed me in the hall. His locks are somewhat grayer and thinner than they were on the morning he disputed with Lady Howard about the vaccination of the noble Sir Reginald, then an infant not much over a year old. My Lady would not have the upper part of the dear child's arm disfigured by the slightest scar, and actually constrained the Doctor to vaccinate the under part which became so irritated with constant rubbing against the poor infant's side, that the sore was not healed until after she died; although little Fred Mansfield's arm, that was vaccinated in the usual place the very same day, healed in a week.

LESTER. (*Rising.*) Woman, you surprise me! I remember the circumstance you mention, distinctly, and so does the Doctor, who but quite recently read both cases for me from a note made in his diary at the time they occurred, where every case, no matter how trifling, connected with his practice for over thirty years, will be found entered minutely.

MEG. And how is dear, good, kind Sir Reginald, and Sarah Waters, that nursed him in foreign lands, after little Fred Mansfield died there? And what became of Nancy Evans, whose old mother still lives in the village, and who, after taking a solemn oath to watch over the dear baby, disappeared from the Manor, after my Lady died, whose foster-sister she was, and who nursed the young child until he was taken from her by Mrs. Mansfield, and carried beyond the seas;

although, with tears and prayers, she begged to be allowed to accompany him ?

LESTER. (*With increasing astonishment, and laying his hand on her shoulder.*) Woman! what is your name? How came you by this knowledge? I must know. What is your name?

MEG. (*Drawing a folded paper from her bosom, and presenting it to LESTER.*) Read this, and you may learn my name and something more besides! But, before opening it, you must pledge me solemnly that you will not divulge its contents to any one save Doctor Harley and the three others named, until the evening before Sir Reginald's birthday, now at the door.

LESTER. (*Taking the paper and handing MEG a chair.*) I promise. Be seated. (*She sits down.*) I shall look over this now, lest I may have something to say to you on it at once. (*Resumes his seat, and, opening the paper, begins to read with interest, culminating in the wildest and most uncontrollable excitement. Leaping to his feet in a tremor of frenzy, and still staring at the paper*). Great heaven! What is this? Ring for Harley! Ho! Harley! Harley! (*Bounding over to MEG, and seizing her by the arm.*) Woman, you're insane! or am I mad? I can read no more! It's a lie! It's a lie! Ring for Harley! (*Sinks into a chair, overcome with the most fearful excitement. MEG rings; but the sound is scarcely heard when the door is burst suddenly open, and the DOCTOR rushes in, in a state of excitement the most extraordinary also.*)

DOCT. (*Dashing up to LESTER, who bounds to his feet again.*) Lester! Lester! The world's coming to an end! Read this! Read this, that has been just sworn to by Waters! (*Thrusting the paper before him.*) Read! read, man! Read!

LESTER. (*Engrossed with his own case, and being, as it were, half beside himself.*) Doctor! Doctor! Look at that woman! Is she mad, or am I mad? It's a lie, Doctor! It's a lie! Read! Read it! (*Endeavoring to attract the DOCTOR's attention to the paper given him by MEG.*)

DOCT. Lester, what has occurred to you? Are we all mad?

(*Both sink into a chair*).

MEG. (*Who observes the whole scene without the slightest discomposure, rising and standing before both the DOCTOR and LESTER.*) Gentlemen, calm yourselves! You are both quite sane, and so am I, and so, doubtless, is Sarah Waters also. Compare both documents carefully! Perhaps one may have some bearing on the other. I have spoken to Sarah lately!

DOCT. True! true! But has the sky fallen?

LESTER. What's the matter, Harley? I see something mysterious has befallen you also! (*Rising.*) Let us all retire to my private study, and try and solve this miraculous case of mine, and yours, too, as you seem to have one. (*Making a sign to MEG.*) Good woman, we shall need you; follow us! [*Exeunt.*

SCENE III.— *The wood. Enter* SIR REGINALD *and* TONY, *conversing.* SIR REGINALD *throws himself on a rustic seat, while* TONY *stands beside him.*

SIR REGINALD. Well, Lightfoot, although I know nothing of that silly teething-brash called love, and notwithstanding what you have now told me, I won't be foiled! But you are certain all this passed between them?

TONY. I was as near them as I am to you, Sir Reginald! It was nothing but billing and cooing, fond adieus, and vows of eternal love!

SIR REGINALD. See to it, Lightfoot! This beggar has crossed my path, and to be candid, I have already had some evidence of the truth of what you now say! You and I have known each other for some time! Look to it! You know!

TONY. Sir Reginald, have I ever failed you?

SIR REGINALD. No! Lightfoot, never! And now, by the way, that I think of it, have you not often told me that you would like to keep an inn?

TONY. (*With sudden interest.*) I have, Sir Reginald. It was always my ambition!

SIR REGINALD. Well, then, let me tell you that I shall turn Capon out of the White Hart immediately.

TONY. As he richly deserves, Sir Reginald, for always siding against you, and having become so great an admirer of this tutor that is now hand and glove with the Doctor and Mr. Lester.

SIR REGINALD. (*Significantly.*) Both of whom are magistrates as well as I am, Lightfoot! Remember that!

TONY. (*Confidently.*) Never fear, Sir Reginald, I'm no novice in these little affairs, as you know.

SIR REGINALD. What is this you were saying of that gypsy woman?

TONY. That she is very poor and hates this Travers, as I have been informed, who is now to be met nightly passing, from the Hermitage to the Grange, through the wood.

SIR REGINALD. You have a hundred pounds at your disposal; but be cautious; and recollect, Lightfoot, I advise nothing, nor do I suggest anything!

TONY. I understand, Sir Reginald! I know what I'm about: and will not rely much upon the friendliness of the Doctor, who said that Whiting should have broken every bone in my body instead of simply giving me a bloody nose the other day.

SIR REGINALD. What has resuscitated that old hag, Waters? Although she nursed me, I have always hated her, for she never seemed to evince the slightest affection for me.

TONY. Oh! the old witch had been ailing for some time, but she's now about again, more lively than ever. The Doctor or the gypsy prescribed something for her lately, for they have both been with her, I hear, and she is now as brisk as can be.

SIR REGINALD. Yes, I knew she had been ill in both mind and body for months, whatever the poor devil has done, and that's why I was surprised to see her bustling about this morning. You may go, now, Lightfoot. You have business to do; and I shall ride over to the Oakes, and perhaps into the village.

TONY. I have business to do, Sir Reginald, and you may consider it just as good as done ! (*Significantly.*)

[*Bows and disappears among the trees.*

SIR REGINALD. (*Solus.*) I have been too precipitate at the Hermitage ! I must retrace my steps, if I would crush this proud, beggarly beauty ! I must come across that old dotard of a father of hers, express my contrition for my hasty conduct regarding him and this lackey, who is now in good hands ! I must ask his permission to return to the Hermitage, so that I may endeavor to make my peace personally with his daughter, whom I could even make Lady Howard sooner than fail ! I shall be able to glean from her own lips how the case actually stands between us. I may, if I find it necessary, make a formal offer of my hand !—my hand, even ! It will be a bold experiment, but should she reject the honor, beyond a shadow of hope, then shall I crush her ! crush her ! crush her into the dust ! (*gesticulating at each pause*) and send her and her father to the door afterwards, without a guinea in their purse, or a roof of their own to shelter them ! But now for the Oakes and the village. I must learn what is said or done regarding this coming fête, whose progress seems to have got so sudden an impetus at the Manor. But all won't do, Master Lester ! You shan't creep into my good graces at the eleventh hour. You go with the rest of them ! (*Suddenly rising and walking away.*)

[*Exit* SIR REGINALD.

END OF ACT II.

ACT III.

SCENE I.—*Room in the Grange, with books, etc.* TRAVERS *seated at a table, with his head resting on his hand, in deep thought.*

TRAVERS. (*Rising and slowly pacing the apartment.*)
There's not a sordid fibre in her soul
To bind her to the chariot-wheels of wealth ;
So here, again, between her heart and mine,

An empty purse can yawn no fatal gulf !
Oh, how I love her for so fierce and proud
A refutation of that cruel lie,
That all the surest shafts of the blind god
Are winged with selfish plumes and tipped with gold !
And how my spirit reels within me still,
Drunk with the nectar of her first warm kiss,
When the soft murmurs of her trembling voice
So filled the chambers of my listening soul,
That all my being into music turned,
And with a sudden, nameless rapture burned !   (*Some one knocks.*)
Come in ! come in !

Enter DOCTOR HARLEY.

DOCT. How do you do, Travers? They told me I'd find you here.

TRAVERS. Doctor, I am delighted to see you. (*They shake hands.*) Be seated. (*Hands a chair. The* DOCTOR *sits.*) You see my shoulder is quite restored. (*Touching one of his shoulders with his hand.*)

DOCT. Only a slight sprain; quite a trifle, Travers.

TRAVERS. So I supposed at the time I slipped, Doctor; but, really, you examined it with such interest last evening that I thought I was more hurt than I had supposed.

DOCT. (*Laughingly.*) Why, yes, I recollect now that I did look rather narrowly at it. But, then, my dear fellow, you must know, to the eye of an old practitioner such as I am, the very simplest cases sometimes present features of great interest. Miss Mortimer sends her compliments, and thanks you for the books and flowers.

TRAVERS. Then, Doctor. I am indebted to you and Miss Mortimer both; to her, for her politeness and consideration, and to you, for being the bearer of what, I must confess, is most gratifying to me.

DOCT. Travers! (*Pauses.*)

TRAVERS. Well, Doctor?

DOCT. Would you mind my calling you "a sly dog?"

TRAVERS. (*Laughing.*) Why, no indeed, Doctor. There is nothing so terrible in it !

DOCT. (*Archly.*) Then, Travers, you are a sly dog; and a very sly one, or old Frank Harley's mistaken ! I heard of the whole affair between you and Sir Reginald at the Hermitage. Mortimer says you behaved nobly; but that he never thought some one you know of was such a "vixen !"—such an "Amazon !" These were his words; although they were accompanied by a very merry twinkle of his eye.

TRAVERS. It was she, Doctor, who behaved nobly, and who treated that titled gambler and libertine as he deserved !

DOCT. But will you believe it ? He has come down off his high horse, and apologized to Mortimer, in the village, for his vile conduct in relation to the whole of you, and asked permission to call again at the Hermitage, in the hope of making his peace with Miss Mortimer ! In short, my dear fellow, he went so far as to intimate that he intended to propose, if he felt there was absolute forgiveness on her part; and you know, Travers, that the family have long been in sore pecuniary straits!

TRAVERS. (*With excitement.*) Let him propose, Doctor! but if I know anything of Miss Mortimer, she will be more explicit with him than she was on the occasion you have spoken of, and give him his *congé* in a manner not to be mistaken.

DOCT. Then, Travers, the family will, I am certain, be embarrassed very seriously, and at once; for you have, I presume, heard that Sir Reginald, by some means or other, has managed to get the Hermitage into his clutches, and can turn them out of it now, at almost any moment he chooses.

TRAVERS. (*Excitedly.*) But have the Mortimers no friends or relatives to aid them in this the hour of their sore distress?

DOCT. Plenty of friends, Travers; but none that I am aware of who are sufficiently wealthy to spare anything like the amount that would relieve the Hermitage of its embarrassments.

TRAVERS. (*Bitterly.*) Now I feel what it is to be poor! and yet, what a monster riches may make a man!

DOCT. Never despair, Travers! Men as poor as you and I have become suddenly rich through some freak of fortune!

TRAVERS. Doctor! in my case it would be a most unaccountable freak of fortune, indeed!

DOCT. I'm not so sure of that! But, let me ask you if you know anything of that Gypsy Meg, more than you have already told me?

TRAVERS. Nothing more, Doctor. Nothing more.

DOCT. Have you not heard, lately, that she is an enemy of yours?

TRAVERS. Well, I had a slight intimation of something of the sort recently; but I really can scarcely believe that she is.

DOCT. I heard it whispered that she was always dogging your steps in and about the wood; and, lest the rumor, if it happened to have reached your ears, should cause you any uneasiness, I dropped in more particularly to say, you may rest satisfied that, though eccentric, the woman is, in my opinion, quite harmless.

TRAVERS. Thank you, Doctor, for your goodness. I think your estimate of this Meg's disposition is correct. I never met her until her arrival here recently; although, within a day or two, she has told me that she knew me in other lands; and that she is an English gypsy, who, during the war, had, without the slightest provocation, been suddenly seized in France as a spy, and thrust into prison, where, not being allowed the privilege of communicating with her friends, she had lain for years and years, until the recent proclamation of peace, when she was set free, an old woman, without ever having had a trial! This I believe to be true; for she speaks French fluently, and knows everything about French prison-life. However, after all, she may be an impostor and dangerous; but I doubt it.

2

DOCT. So do I, Travers. By the way, Lester tells me you have been long promising to take a drive into town with him. We are going in immediately, and would like you to join us. You can ride with either of us, for I always take my own trap, having generally some calls to make on the road. We mostly spend the evening with the solicitors in Clifford street, who are two noble fellows and old friends of ours. You promised to make them a visit the time you and they dined with me. They like you amazingly, and will be delighted if you spend a night with us beneath their magnificent and hospitable roof.

TRAVERS. I was very much pleased with both these gentlemen, and shall feel great pleasure in visiting them with you and Mr. Lester at any time; but I trust you may both make it convenient to leave this before the coming fête, as I should like to remain in the city until it is over.

DOCT. Nonsense, Travers! Lester is constrained to be here on that day, to make explanations and give up his trust; and we, his friends, are not going to desert him at a moment so critical. Out of friendship and respect for him, my dear fellow, we must all be present! Even the Mortimers must be there; for you must know that, until Lester formally relinquishes his office and places certain parchments in the hands of the heir, which he won't do until he has said his say, Sir Reginald will have no more power at the Manor than I have. That's all arranged; and let me tell you the people of the Grange and many of the élite of the village are going.

TRAVERS. Well, Doctor, if you are quite satisfied that the attendance you refer to will not be construed into any respect for this Sir Reginald, but be set down to the proper account, I cannot see any objection to my being present, or any of the friends of Mr. Lester; as we all can leave the Manor when the transfer is made, and just before this Howard makes a speech that he has, I learn, been studying of late most assiduously.

DOCT. That's right, Travers! I'm on foot. Will you take a turn in the wood, for a few moments? (*Both rising.*)

TRAVERS. With all my heart! 　　　　　　　　　　　[*Exeunt.*

———

SCENE II.—*Apartment in the Hermitage.* SUSAN *busily engaged arranging it. Statue on the mantel-piece.*

SUSAN. (*Pausing suddenly.*) I'll brain that Dick Whiting with this (*raising a small feather-duster*) the next time he dares to kiss me on the stairs! The way I'm worried with that wretch is enough to make me go into a nunnery, if I only knew my catechism! I hate the very sight of him! so I do, handsome and all as he is; but I suppose it's not the poor fellow's fault! (*Looking admiringly in a glass.*) And much as I detest him, I wish he was here now to take down that heavy Columbus, there, (*pointing at a bronze statue on the mantel-piece*), that wants to be dusted so!

Enter DICK, *who had been peeping unnoticed in at the door.*

DICK. And here I am, Susy dear! for I was just a thinkin' that he wanted a dustin', and that you wouldn't be able to take'n down. (*Going to remove the statue.*)

SUSY. (*Raising her duster.*) Just leave it there, Mr. Impiddence! for now that I recollect it, I had it down yesterday; and besides, you followed me! And what's more, you took me unawares on the stairs!

DICK. Well, Susy dear! do you take me for a parson as could pass such a pair of sweet lips within three inches on him, without tryin' on 'em with a will?

SUSY. (*Emphatically.*) Dick Whiting, I hate you!

DICK. I know, Susy; but if you don't love any one else, I'm not agoin' to gi'd in for that!

SUSY. (*With quickness.*) Ha! you monster of jealousy! who else do I love that you are hinting at'?

DICK. (*Coaxingly.*) No one in the world, Suky, but your own Dick, that worships the very ground you walk on; and that, one day or other, will make you his wife, in the best silk gown and shawl that's to be found in the village.

SUSY. (*Dusting away*) Don't be so sure of that, Master Whiting; and besides, I never intend to marry—like my dear, sweet mistress!

DICK. If you're the purtiest, you're the most provokin'est on 'em; and what would you say, Susy, the next time I went into Lunnon, if you heerd on me takin' some one with sweet blue eyes and lovely hair, just like your'n, to Greenwich?

SUSY. (*Contemptuously.*) A fig for your London, Dick! See what it has done for Sir Reginald, who now, I hear, is going to ask Miss Alice to take his poor wizzen heart off his hands, that's as hard as a flint and as cold as the north pole. But she's not going to have any one, Dick; although more's the pity; for I know of some one and she who would make a splendid pair!

DICK. I know who you mean, Suky; and he is summat when compared with that ugly customer at the Manor, who is now agoin' to have the upper hand of the whole on us.

SUSY. (*Laying down her duster.*) I only wish you had given him the drubbing you gave that valet of his: for he deserved it richly, for daring to give a cut of his whip to you, who never did a wrong act in your life, and who is one of the best and most true-hearted lads in the whole of Kent (*stopping suddenly, on perceiving* DICK'S *delight*), that is, as I have heard them say.

DICK. (*With happy earnestness.*) Suky, dear, don't put back the tide that was settin' in so strong atords me in your heart; for, although I'm a poor lad I'm an honest un, and if it pleases you, I'll break every bone in Sir Reginald's body the next time I lay my eyes on him near the White Hart.

SUSY. (*Laughing, and with more tenderness.*) No! no! Dick, you mustn't do that; for they might put you in jail, and then I'd have no one to take down Columbus for me! (*Looking at* DICK *archly.*) But tell me, how did Sir Reginald get the Hermitage into his power?

DICK. Well, you know, when the minin' and the other speculations failed, the master was obliged to keep mor gagin' the property until he could raise no more money on it; when Sir Reginald, as it joined on to his own estates, made some sort of a bargain with those as holds the mortgages, which are now about run out, that they would turn them over to him, for a certain sum, on which he agreed to pay interest in the meantime, when his own property came into his hands.

SUKY. Yes, and so that he might have a claw on my sweet mistress besides! (*Looking out of the window.*) But here she is, and her father, coming, after their walk, so you must go at once! They may come up here!

DICK. (*Approaching her winningly.*) Well, if I must, I must! But before I go, will you (*extending his open arms*), Suky dear?

SUSY. Dick! Don't be a fool! But will you go then; for I'd almost sooner do anything than that you should be found here by them!

DICK. On the spot, Suky dear!

SUKY. Well, don't take me unawares, then!

(DICK *fancying he hears approaching footsteps, bounds forward, and kissing her rapidly, disappears at once.*

SUSY. (*In feigned surprise.*) Well, did your ever! What a good-for-nothing, brazen wretch, not to give me a moment's notice! It's almost as bad as the stairs! If I don't be even with you next time, Master Dick Whiting, I'm not here! (*Looking in the glass.*) See the way he has left my cap! I would not let Miss Alice see it in this state for the world! So, as I think I hear her father and herself approaching, I'll be off and set it to rights in my own chamber.   [*Exit* SUSAN.

Enter ALICE *and* MORTIMER, *conversing.*

MORTIMER. Yes, my dear, as I have already told you, he made a most ample apology to me in the village, where I happened to encounter him accidentally. (*Both seat themselves.*)

ALICE. But has he made one to Mr. Travers, papa?

MORT. That I cannot say. I may observe, however, that he admitted to me his remarks regarding Mr. Travers were quite uncalled for; and further, if I must be more explicit with you, he declared that he had unfortunately lost his temper when he saw you and the tutor standing together at the window on such apparently intimate terms.

ALICE. It seems he was jealous, then!

MORT. So it would appear, my dear. But as he has asked my permission, which I accorded, to call again and endeavor to make his peace with you personally, you shall learn what he has to say, from his own lips. I may, however, as well remark, that I think he intends to propose; for he told me, distinctly, that it was his love for you that had betrayed him into the excess of which he had been guilty.

ALICE. (*With scornful vehemence, rising from her seat.*)
His love! Oh! can that holiest of words
Be ever true or bright or pure again
When once pronounced by such polluted lips?
His love! Ohr! never has his sordid soul
Throbbed with a single pulse akin to love,
Much less with the great ecstasy itself!
Whate'er his plea, I never shall be his!
E'en though a royal diadem he wore,
And I but begged my bread from door to door!

MORT. Then are we undone indeed! for well I know this roof above our heads is doomed!

ALICE. And what of it, papa? I am young, and, thanks to you and my dear sainted mother, I am well educated ; and, even now, am seeking a situation as governess in some London family ; for I may as well inform you that I have already advertised in two of the most prominent journals, and am hourly in expectation of the offer of some engagement.

MORT. Alice, dear child, I was not aware of this! (*With great emotion.*) But pray heaven a kind Providence may avert the calamity of our separation for even a single day, until it occurs in the ordinary course of nature. But although I have hitherto presumed that much that has been said of Sir Reginald's character is exaggerated, I must now leave you to act for yourself, lest my sore needs warp my judgment. But here he comes! That surely was his voice! I shall leave you alone. May all good angels guide you! [*Exit* MORTIMER.

Enter SUSAN.

SUS. Sir Reginald Howard, Miss Alice.

ALICE. (*Standing with her hand resting on the back of a chair, and with her head slightly inclined.*) Show Sir Reginald in. [*Exit* SUSAN.

Enter SIR REGINALD, *with well-feigned humility.*

SIR REGINALD. (*Bowing profoundly.*) Miss Mortimer, I am here by permission of your best friend, your father, so that I may have an opportunity of expressing to you personally my deep contrition for the rudeness and injustice into which I allowed my temper to betray me beneath this roof so recently, and to ask your forgiveness for the same.

ALICE. (*Pointing to a chair at some distance, and seating herself in the one by which she had been standing.*) Take a chair, Sir Reginald (*he seats himself, bowing*), and let me say, briefly, that, in view of the apology you now make, you have my full forgiveness for the offence to which you refer, if that avail you anything.

SIR REG. (*A little disconcerted.*) You are generous, Miss Mortimer; but I trust you are not totally insensible of the fact that your good opinion avails me much, and that without it I should be the most miserable fellow alive!

ALICE. (*Calmly.*) I said "forgiveness," Sir Reginald; a word which I beg you will weigh in its true balance, and not freight beyond its endurance!

SIR REG. (*With a little tartness.*) Well, "forgiveness," if you will have it so, Miss Mortimer; yet I trust you comprehend that I mean something more.

ALICE. In truth, Sir Reginald, I am at a loss to divine what you may mean farther; and the more so, as I have reached the limits of what you are good enough to term my generosity.

SIR REG. (*With an effort.*) Well, Miss Mortimer, as you do not choose to comprehend me, I shall come to the point at once; and, in fact, may as well say that I am persuaded you would make an admirable Lady Howard, and as I am now coming into my immense fortune, I am here to lay both it and my name at your feet! (*Rising and advancing towards* ALICE, *who also rises, but with a motion of her hand which arrests him.*)

ALICE. (*With composure and distinctness.*) You are frank, Sir Reginald; and it would be discourteous and disingenuous in me were I to say that I am not impressed with the high honor you would confer upon me. I must, however, meet you with the openness that your frankness deserves, and state at the outset that my heart has already been disposed of to another; so that you may perceive at a glance I can never stand in any other relation to you than that which I occupy at the present moment.

SIR REG. (*With suppressed rage and mortification.*) Perhaps, after all, fair lady, my wealth and family do not meet your exalted aspirations!

ALICE. (*Coolly.*) Your family is no better than mine, Sir Reginald; and as for wealth, there are other considerations which I place immeasurably above it!

SIR REG. Or perhaps I'm not sufficiently learned or romantic to win your fastidious affections! If so, I shall at once take to books, or twanging the moonlight guitar at the edge of the wood close by, in worship of the inaccessible divinity enshrined here!

ALICE. (*Smiling most provokingly.*) In good truth, Sir Reginald, any change in your occupations and mode of life would be of infinite advantage to you: although, as for books and music, I fear they are somewhat out of your line.

SIR REG. (*Unable to contain himself.*) Miss Mortimer will excuse me if I am not constrained to take up either for a livelihood!

ALICE. (*Laughing outright.*) It is, really, most fortunate for you, Sir Reginald!

SIR REG. Indeed! And why, pray?

ALICE. (*Still laughing.*) You must ask some one more versed in these matters than I, Sir Reginald!

SIR REGINALD. That lackey at the Grange, for instance!

ALICE. (*With bitter hilarity.*) Yes! if you only have the courage!

SIR REG. (*Bounding to his feet.*) What do you mean by courage, Miss Alice Mortimer?

ALICE. The meaning is known to every true gentleman; I'm not surprised at your query!

SIR REG. (*Rushing towards the door.*) This second outrage has been premeditated, I see! (*Pausing on the threshold.*) Listen, Alice Mortimer! Before this coming week closes, you and your father shall be without house or home, and without a shilling in your pocket, save what you may obtain from the hand of charity! [*Exit* SIR REGINALD.

ALICE. (*Solus.*) Now indeed the die is doubly cast! (*Rings.*)

Enter SUSAN.

SUS. Well, Miss Alice, you rang.

ALICE. Yes. Tell papa I'm alone!   [*Exit* SUSAN.

Enter MORTIMER.

MORT. (*Sinking into a chair.*) You need not explain, my child! I can divine it all! Sir Reginald just rushed past me in the hall, without saying a word, and absolutely thrust me aside out of his way, as it were, and disappeared before I could resent the outrage!

ALICE. (*Indignantly.*) The coward! The scoundrel! Would that Dick or Mr. Travers had witnessed the dastardly act!

MORTIMER. (*Rising.*) But come, my dear daughter! the crisis I so long dreaded and struggled against is upon us at last! Let us look over those papers I was speaking about. They are in the library!

[Exeunt.

END OF ACT III.

ACT IV.

SCENE I.—*The wood.* DICK *and* MIKE *meet accidentally.*

DICK. Is that you, Mike? How goes it, lad? Do ee know I've been just a thinkin' that's a good job for both on us, as we beant gen'lemen!

MIKE. (*Drawing himself up humorously with a look of importance.*) Mr. Richard Whitin', Esquire, knight and barrow-knight, answer for yourself! But recollect you're talkin' to an O'Grady, minny of whose relashuns, in the Ould Sod, held high stashuns in Ninety-eight, for at laste fifteen minnits by the docther's watch!

DICK. That be a main short while, Mike; but I suppose it was quite long enough for some on 'em. (*Laughing.*)

MIKE. (*Tenderly.*) Ah, sure, man alive, that's what makes me so melancholy, and fond of a dhrop, wid a bade on it, now and then. But, for that matther, I was always a tindher-hearted boy; for often me poor mother tould me—the heavens be her bed—that whin I wasn't more then five years ould, I'd knock your brains out wid a lump of a shtone, if I only saw you but hurtin' a fly! But, tell me, hadn't yez it, down at the Harmitage there, hot and heavy of late?

DICK. Ay, sure, lad; and they all gid it to'n in style. Miss Alice turned'n off body and bones, with all his great fortin, and Master Travers was near gid'n somethin' wuss then I gid that jimcrack as waits on his highness!

MIKE. The only pity is, that that dancin'-masther of his is so small; not bein' much bigger than that ould gypsy, Meg, that'll do some damage here yet, or I'm mistaken; for Dick, mind you, me boy, her race is not to be depinded upon; although sorra bit of me b'leeves there's a single dhrop of rale gypsy blood in her body.

DICK. I don't know, Mike, what to make on her, for she beant with any tribe, and knows no one here as cares for her, but old granny Evans, Nancy's mother, as is yet alive and keeps t'other side of the village. She picked her up, and lets her stay with her; for, arter all, a woman's a woman and desarvin' of summat more than a man.

MIKE. (*Romantically.*) Dick, if my heart wasn't bruck thirteen years ago by a Limerick girl, I'd agree wid you; but whin I think of the way I was sarved, and the nine mouths I spint in Clonmel Jail for the little difference I had wid the other blaggard that came betune her and me, and that she married the day afther I was put in, I wondher sometimes why I don't bury meself in a monasthry and spind the remaindher of me days in pace and plinty!

DICK. I'll lay you a wager I know where your comin' from, Mike.

MIKE. Where? Tell me, avourneen!

DICK. From the snares!

MIKE. How do you know?

DICK. There's the foot of a rabbit stickin' out on your pocket!

MIKE. Blur and turf! Dick, and so there is! (*Stuffing the foot hastily in again.*) And it's well you got a peep of it; for here comes Misther Lesther, and I wouldn't for the world that he saw it; for he doesn't b'leeve there's an honester fella in the whole county; and no more suspects me of settin' a snare then the man of the moon!

Enter LESTER *from a bypath,* DICK *and* MIKE *touch their hats.*

DICK. Good-mornin', Mr. Lester. Fine day, Mr. Lester.

MIKE. The top o' the mornin' to yer honor, and long life to you!

LESTER. (*Cheerfully.*) Ah! Whiting, is that you? How are Miss Alice and Mr. Mortimer? Well, Mike, how come on the rabbit-pies over at the White Hart? They say you have them every day or so now.

DICK. Master and Miss Alice be main well, Mister Lester, thankee, hopin' you're the same.

MIKE. (*Avoiding the allusion to the pies.*) Yis, indeed, yer honor; and wasn't that a narra escape that the sweet young lady had some short time ago? Her neck was in danger!

LESTER. (*Laughing.*) Not in half so much danger, I fancy, Mike, as the necks of some of the poor rabbits about here. But you have not told me how the pies come on.

MIKE. Ah! the Lord love you, Misther Lesther! and it's you that will have your joke; although, of coorse, there's minny a thing bilt, baked, and roasted over there, that poor Mike O'Grady knows little about!

LESTER. Very likely, Mike! In fact, I suppose you have never set a snare in this wood, nor seen a rabbit, nor tasted a bit of a rabbit-pie since you came to the White Hart!

MIKE. (*Musingly.*) Now stop! Let me see, Misther Lesther! I don't want to tell a lie! Yis, now that I remimber it, we had a pie, I think, about four year ago, out of a present that was made by some one or other to Misther Capon; and, sthrange enough it was, that the only rabbit I ever recollect seein' in this place, I saw the very day afther, crossin' the road outside the wood there.

(*Here* DICK, *perceiving the leg of the rabbit again protruding from* MIKE'S *pocket. begins to gesticulate warningly to him, and laughs out right, as he does not take the hint.*)

LESTER. Whiting seems amused at your story, Mike, and so am I: but what is this? (*Catching a glimpse of the leg of the rabbit, and drawing out the whole animal, which he holds up before* MIKE.) Eh! Mike!

MIKE. (*Turning suddenly round to* DICK, *in feigned astonishment mingled with admiration. Lifting his hands. Laughing spasmodically.*) Ha! ha! ha! ha!—Well! if that doesn't bate all! How the divil did he get it in there, Misther Lesther, without my knowin' it? (*Looking amazed, round at his pocket, and thrusting one hand into it.*) Ah! but you're the play boy. (*Turning to* DICK, *who enjoys the whole affair.*) And that's what you were laughin' at, and no wondher; for it's the cleverest thrick that ever was played on me! But I see through it all!

LESTER. (*Still holding up the rabbit, and amused beyond measure. Turning to* DICK.) Well, Whiting, it appears that you're the culprit in this case.

DICK. Well, Mr. Lester!——Dash my——

MIKE. (*Suddenly interrupting him.*) Now, Dick, tell the thruth! But hould your tongue and let me do it for you! Well, you see (*addressing* LESTER), Misther Lesther, he always threatened to have a joke on me about a rabbit at the expinse of me karracther; knowin' how hou

2*

est I was, as well as partiklar, swarin' that he'd prove, some time or other, that I knew more about the poor innocent cratshures in the wood here, then I let on.

DICK. (*In amazement.*) Oh! Mike!

MIKE. (*Hastily clapping his hand on* DICK's *mouth.*) Hould your tongue now, 'till I'm done! I'm sure Misther Lesther will forgive you, and so will I; for it's nothin' afther all! Well, sir, you see (*turns to* LESTER), he was boastin' yestherday of a fine rabbit that he was made a present of in the village: so, sez he, last night when it rained so hard, and we were takin' somethin' together over at the White Hart, will you lind me the loan of that coat of your's, for mine is so thin, and I'll bring it up in the mornin' when I'm goin' to the Grange? And welcome, sez I, never suspectin' anythin'. So, not five minnits ago, while I was looking about here for them turkeys of ours, in my shirt sleeves, I meets him wid the coat on his arm; and, puttin' it on me without noticin' anythin' wrong, will you b'leeve me, Misther Lesther, that, only for you, I might have taken that fine, fat rabbit home without my knowin' a haporth about it, whin he'd pull it out of my pocket before the whole of them, and have a nice laugh at me, that was always so much agin poachin' or even handlin' a snare!

LESTER. (*Laughing heartily at* MIKE's *innocent countenance and ingenuity.*) Here, Mike, take the rabbit! You deserve it! I wonder how they ever manage to hang one of your countrymen. (*Hands the rabbit to* MIKE, *who takes it.*)

MIKE. Thankee, Misther Lesther, and now that I have come by it honestly, I'll enjoy a bit of it!

DICK. (*In utter astonishment.*) Well, dash my buttons! if ever——

MIKE. (*Again interrupting him.*) Och! man, where's the use of sayin' any more on the subject? Sure naither Misther Lesther or me thinks anythin' about it! It was only a joke; and I will say that the divil a betther one was ever played on honest Mike O'Grady! Come along, and help me to look afther them turkeys.

LESTER. (*Turning away and resuming his walk.*) And the snares, Mike! (*Good humoredly.*)

MIKE. Oh! Misther Lesther, you needn't hint that to him; for I'm sure he came by the rabbit honestly! Come along, Dick!

[*Exeunt. All disappear among the trees.*

SCENE II.—*Private apartment in the Manor.* SIR REGINALD *pacing it with a dissatisfied air.*

SIR REG. So she has shown her hand at last, in a manner not to be mistaken, and has absolutely ventured to make me a subject of ridicule to my very face! Well, I think I shall be even with her yet, and the low-born lackey who has dared to step between us! I have seen her advertisement, and have written this letter (*taking a letter from a table and glancing at the superscription*) to Letitia, 84 Clifford street, London; directly opposite where those close-fisted, beggarly solicitors live. She shall answer this advertisement instantly, as I have here instructed her, and betray this proud beauty into her establishment, on the plea of needing her services as a governess. She is to entice her to town at once, by intimations of the most liberal character, and, when once beneath her roof, detain her, at all hazards, until I drop in on her accidentally, which, rely upon it, will be a very few minutes after her arrival! I shall look to that part of the business! If I happen to discover her there, it will be no fault of mine! When she finds where she is, perhaps she may come to terms and accept my hand; for now I swear I could marry her, if only to be avenged of her for the manner in which she has sneered at me! Letitia knows what she's about! So that if this supercilious beggar does not consent to become mine in the bonds of wedlock, which I shall make heavy, galling chains to her, she shall return to the Hermitage with a cloud on her fair fame at least; for I shall disclose, adroitly, where I happened to find her! But Lightfoot knows all about it; I have already taken him into my confidence on the subject. (*Rings.*)

Enter TONY.

TONY. (*Bowing.*) What's your pleasure, Sir Reginald?

SIR REG. This is the letter, Lightfoot. (*Handing it to him.*) You proceed to 84 with it at once. Don't spare horseflesh. You can be there in a couple of hours. Be sure and tell Letitia to make liberal promises. I have told her to write while you remain, so that you may mail the letter for the Hermitage yourself.

TONY. I understand, Sir Reginald; and know the road pretty well. The letter in answer to the advertisement will be here within a few hours, perhaps as soon as I am myself; and of course they will be on the lookout at the Hermitage, now, for every mail.

SIR REG. But be careful, Lightfoot, that no one knows you have left for town. In fact, you must so disguise yourself before you leave the Manor, that even I should not know you if I happened to meet you on the highway. Be cautious, Lightfoot! Remember the White Hart! and recollect there is not a minute to lose!

TONY. In ten minutes from this, Sir Reginald, I shall be on the road, as honest a looking countryman as ever you laid your eyes on; and, rely upon it, no grass shall grow under my horse's feet. [*Exit* TONY.

SIR REG. (*Solus.*) That Lightfoot is invaluable to me! It is well that he is as true as steel! If he were not, he might embarrass me notwithstanding all my rank and wealth! There are one or two little things that he knows of! Well, it was his hand, not mine, that did the work! Pshaw! What a pretty thing to be thinking of just now, with the hour of my triumph at hand! And besides, supposing this selfsame

Miss Mortimer does make a fuss; what business had she to be in such a place? Why, the thing is as plain as a pikestaff; and with Letitia and Lightfoot, as well as my fortune and title, at my back, I can bid her defiance. But I must now seek some retired place in the open air, and test my voice with that speech of mine, which I have committed to memory, and am to deliver from the Manor steps, for the benefit of those vulgarians and others who are constrained to assemble in my honor, before a great many suns have set! [*Exit* SIR REGINALD.

SCENE III.—*The Hermitage.* ALICE *and* TRAVERS *conversing on the moonlit lawn.*

TRAVERS. Yes! dearest, your father, like yourself, has generously consented to sacrifice so much worth and beauty to so much poverty. Of course, I shall feel deeply our temporary separation; but London, beloved, is not at the antipodes; and I shall write daily and see you often, until our fortunate star peeps above the horizon.

ALICE. My hope, dear Stanhope, is, that you shall soon be able to procure some position in town, which, united with mine, if this letter I have just received lead to an engagement, may enable us to make some provision for my poor father, who is now sorely tried indeed, and no longer young.

TRAVERS. It shall be my first care, dearest; and, as you are aware, I shall be in the city, and at the house of the solicitors I spoke of, I may be able to obtain some information on this all-important point from some of these gentlemen.

ALICE. You leave early to-morrow with Mr. Lester, he informs me. The Doctor and I start in the afternoon, as he cannot be ready sooner. You will all three meet at your friends, while poor I shall have a solitary *tête-à-tête* with my crusty old aunt, after I have seen the people at No. 84, which Mr. Lester informs me must be nearly or quite opposite the solicitors; so that, after all, I may get a glimpse of you. The Doctor will drop me at the door of Mrs. Mayfield, as she signs herself; from whence, after seeing the lady, I shall proceed to my aunt's residence, No. 160, close by, where you can call upon me early the next morning, and learn how I have succeeded, as, before returning to the Hermitage, I shall remain a day or two with my aunt.

TRAVERS. I shall fly to you early, and learn how it has fared with you. But remember, dearest, we are now all pledged to stand by Mr. Lester on the day he gives up his trust to this Howard, and that as, under any circumstance, you will be obliged to return to the Hermitage immediately, you must manage to be among the ladies present on the occasion.

ALICE. Then you approve fully my intention of accepting this position, should I find it a desirable one?

TRAVERS. (*With warmth and emphasis, while gazing lovingly on* ALICE.)
Yes, dearest, I applaud that high resolve
To seize the adverse spokes in Fortune's wheel,
And struggle to arrest their fatal course,
E'en with these fingers now so soft and fair,
(Takes her fingers fondly).
That Labor's self might almost blush to soil!
Wealth is not necessarily happiness!
Oft the true palace has a sanded floor;
While Greatness in a gilded hovel pines,
Where the tossed pillow never shows at dawn
The one deep impress left by sweet repose.
In the stern school in which I have been taught,
I've learned to love the humbler walks of life;
Although Ambition sometimes will intrude,
And almost scale the bulwarks of my peace.

ALICE. How truly do you say, "Wealth is not necessarily happiness."
And why? Because it cannot purchase peace of mind or love! If we
are poor, Stanhope, when we are made one in the sight of heaven we
shall be no poorer; for I trust we have within us that which is beyond
all riches! But where, if this moment you had the power of a magi-
cian, would you make our home?

TRAVERS. (*With passionate inspiration, while gently relinquishing her
hand.*)
Beside some winding river that is flowing
Clear, cool, and gently through a sunny vale,
As though it were a liquid west-wind blowing
A sort of luscious, lazy, silvery gale
Between two odorous banks with cowslips glowing
In knots of tangled gold, deep-tinged and pale,
And morn-tipped daisies, sprinkling brakes of wildwood—
The fairy haunts of memory, love, and childhood:
There, in a nook, with beauty ever beaming—
A mine of woodland jewels, lit with showers
That leave the wooded dell with incense teeming,
As though it were the passion-time of flowers—
A nook where Autumn nods in golden dreaming,
And blue-eyed Spring comes in her first bright hours,
Tripping along to robin-redbreast measures,
Beneath a fragrant store of primrose treasures—
A sylvan temple on whose em'rald altar
Sweet Nature spreads her offerings to the Sun,
While thrill the raptures of her warbling psalter,
Not doling out her riches one by one
With a spare hand that ever seems to falter,
But letting them in wild profusion run,

As though her lap were heaped with each rare token,
    And on that spot her apron-strings had broken !

ALICE. (*Enraptured.*)   Oh ! dearest, dearest **Stanhope**, I'm en-
chanted.

TRAVERS. (*Continuing.*)
    Be patient !   In this dewy glimpse of Aidenn,
    In a sweet little gypsy of a cot,
    White as a dove, low-eaved, and woodbine-laden—
    A sort of thatch-and-stone " Forget-me-not "—
    There should we make our home.

ALICE. (*Moved to ecstasy.*)   Cease ! dearest, **cease !**
Such eloquence and dreams o'erpower my soul !
And more—thou hast reversed ambition's flight,
And turned it downwards, till mine eyes have caught
The silv'ry down, 'neath its descending wing,
From which far softer pillows may be made
Than from the harsh ascending upper plumes !
But wheresoe'er thy footsteps soon may lead,
Mine shall their faithful shadow ever be.
And though I leave thee now, for a brief space,
To mingle with the city's busy throng,
I leave my heart with thee——

TRAVERS. Beloved one !
And, in return, fill the sweet void with mine
Which, like the dove that left the ark of yore,
Has now gone forth, to dwell with me no more !

ALICE. Come, let us return to my father. We have yet much to **speak**
of. (*Taking* TRAVERS's *arm.*)

TRAVERS. As you will, dearest ! [*Exeunt.   They enter the Hermitage.*

SCENE IV.—*The White Hart.   Enter* MIKE, *emerging from the door
    with some snares and a rabbit-skin in his hands.*

MIKE. (*Holding up the skin and admiring it.*) Oh ! but you were the
bewty !   Four pounds and three-quarters and spatther'd wid **fat !**   Let
me see !   Not countin' hares or **parthridges**, I think this is !—No !—
Yis !—There was seven the week afore last ! and then three times nine
is forty-two ! Och ! what am I ravin' about ? Thirty-six, I mane !
Begorra, I was near forgettin' my multiplicashun table !   Howsomever,
it's no matther.   I had my share of them ; and will give them a partin'
salute wid these (*shaking the snares*), for I suppose that we'll all soon
have to bid good-by to the wood, as well as the White Hart.

Enter DICK.

DICK. I thought you was talkin' to some one, Mike, for I heerd your
voice just now.

MIKE. And so I was, me bouchal! and to a very great friend of mine. the two first letthers of whose name is Mike O'Grady.

DICK. (*Pointing to the rabbit-skin.*) Was he fat?

MIKE. (*Holding up the skin.*) It's my belief that it was his fat choked him, instead of the snare! But what news have you for me?

DICK. Good news, Mike. Miss Alice has got a fine situation in London, or at least she's sure to get'n; for a letter has comed, and she's goin' up this eveniu' to see about'n. Suky says the letter is very civil, and tells her to call, no matter how late she may get into the city. She will stop at her aunt's, the proud old lady's; but won't go see her until she knows all about the situation and makes the bargain, for the master says she'll be again her goin' out as a governess; and try and persuade her off it, unless she tells her everything is settled and no backin' out. The Doctor is goin' into the city, and will drive her to the number that's on the letter, somewhere in Clifford street, and but a short distance from her aunt's. But it seems to me as if everybody was a goin' in to-day, for I just heerd that Mr. Lester and Master Travers are a goin'. I suppose Mr. Lester wants to see the solicitors afore he gives the estates up to Sir Reginald.

Enter CAPON. *Standing in the doorway.*

CAPON. I heerd what you say regardin' Miss Alice and the rest on 'em, Dick, and suppose this is the beginnin' of the grand break up! Well, wherever she may go, she has the good-will and the blessin' of old Ned Capon; for a sweeter creetur doesn't walk in shoe-leather to-day.

MIKE. (*Half seriously.*) Be the mortial man! I feel as if I could crunch a pound of cast-steel betune me jaws! I tell you what! I have lived here for a good minny years, and feel a little soft about lavin'. What, then, must Misther Capon there feel, who was born benathe this very roof, and who lost all that was near and dear to him undher it? Begorra! I have a grate noshun, no matther what comes of me, to give the Docthor a job at the Manor, before the goin's on comminces, near as we're to them!

DICK. There's no use in that, Mike! It will not make things better. But, as I feel warm and weary and thirsty, let us all go in and try a mug of ale; for I suppose we shan't be able to take many more together in the White Hart. [*Exeunt.*

SCENE V.—LETITIA'S *House, London. A showily furnished apartment in it.*

VOICE. (*Without.*) This way, miss! This way, if you please, while I take your card to my mistress.

Enter ALICE, *in a travelling dress.*

ALICE. (*With surprise and disappointment.*) Altogether too showily dressed a servant, I should say! I trust she does not reflect the taste of her mistress in any degree! (*Looking about her uneasily.*) But, really, there seems to be a good deal of expensive vulgarity displayed here! I don't like the place! The air is oppressive, and I fear I shall never be able to make common cause with those who are content to breathe it habitually. (*Takes a seat beside a table upon which, amongst other things, there lies a book marked with a small, pearl-handled dagger, used as a paper-knife. Opens the book and reads.*) "The Phantom Highwayman, or the Blood-stained Hand. A Tragedy!" (*Turns over a few leaves and reads again.*) "And stabs the false Belinda to the heart!" (*While replacing the dagger, closing the book, and laying it down again.*) "Angels and ministers of grace defend us!" The home of the sensational drama also! Ah! Mrs. Mayfield (*shaking her head and smiling languidly*), I fear our acquaintance will be of but very short duration indeed! However, we shall see. (*Hears sounds of approaching footsteps.*) But here she comes, I presume!

Enter LETITIA, *extravagantly and gaudily dressed.*

LETITIA. (*Advancing familiarly, while* ALICE *rises, and extending her hand cordially, which* ALICE *takes coldly.*) Miss Mortimer, let me give you welcome, my dear! I am glad my note found you so speedily, and that you are now here. It was very kind of you, my dear, to pay such prompt attention to it.

ALICE. Thank you, Mrs. Mayfield. As the affair was one of business, I considered it best to dispose of it at once.

LETITIA. (*Winningly.*) It was very good of you, my dear; but as you must be slightly fatigued, at least won't you lay your bonnet aside and allow me to offer you a glass of wine before we speak on other matters?

ALICE. (*With growing suspicion.*) No, thank you, I am not fatigued in the slightest. I am now on my way to my aunt's, and have only been just dropped here to apprise you of my arrival, as you expressed a desire I should do so the moment I reached the city.

LETITIA. (*Eagerly.*) And is your carriage waiting, my dear?

ALICE. Oh! no. I came up with a friend of our family; and have now only a very short distance to walk.

LETITIA. (*With ill-bred persistency.*) Then, my dear, let me prevail on you to take even a single sip of wine, as your spirits seem somewhat depressed, and as it will cheer you while we make arrangements as to salary and so forth.

ALICE. (*Immovably and with some disgust.*) You really must excuse me, Mrs. Mayfield. (*A new idea striking her.*) And you will conceive, readily, that before I can enter into any final arrangement in this matter, I shall first have to consult my aunt. We shall both, however, call upon you in the morning.

LETITIA. (*With a gesture of impatience and a sudden alteration of voice.*) I should suppose, Miss Mortimer, that there is but very little to consult your aunt about in this case. You advertised for a situation as governess in a respectable family, and, I presume, before you did so, you had made up your mind pretty fully to accept the position when it offered.

ALICE. (*Annoyed and slightly alarmed.*) Very true, madam, but it may not follow that I shall snatch at the first that happens to be presented for my acceptance! In the meantime, however (*rising*), and while thanking you for the preference you have given me, I shall take my leave, and consult with my relative on the subject.

LETITIA. (*Rising also. Aside.*) You are not gone yet, my pretty dear! (*To* ALICE, *with feigned carelessness.*) Well, Miss Mortimer, I hope I shall have the pleasure of seeing you and your aunt to-morrow. But, before you go, will you allow me to ask you if you know a lady in your village named—named—(*Pauses and reflects for an instant. Suddenly.*) Oh! will you excuse me for a single moment? I have got it on my tablets in the next room.

ALICE. Certainly!

LETITIA. Thank you! (*Aside.*) I wish you had tasted that wine!
[*Exit* LETITIA, *closing the door behind her.*

ALICE. (*Solus.*) I have been ill at ease! Yes, and am so still! There is something about this Mrs. Mayfield that I do not like! Something that excites suspicion and disgust! Yes, and even creates alarm! I shall never be tempted to accept any engagement at her hands! Her dress and manners are not those of a lady; and everything about this place (*looking around her*) exhales a strange, sickly odor which almost overpowers me! But why does she delay? I am anxious to regain the open air! How oppressive this apartment is becoming. I shall open the door and leave it ajar until she returns, so that I may breathe more freely. (*Approaches the door, but starts in the wildest horror and dismay on finding it securely locked or fastened on the outside.*) Great God! I am locked in! I am lost! (*Flies to the windows, in a state of terrible excitement, but finds them secured with iron bars.*) Iron bars! Help! Help! Oh, God! I've been betrayed! Help! Help! (*Cries aloud.*)

Enter SIR REGINALD, *on tiptoe, through a secret door, which, unperceived by* ALICE, *opens and closes softly behind him in the wainscot.*

SIR REGINALD. (*With a leer of triumph.*) Help is at hand! (ALICE *starts at the sound of his voice, and perceives him with a look of horror and dismay; while he in feigned astonishment recognizes her, as it were, for the first time.*) What! Is it you?

ALICE. (*Fathoming the plot in a moment.*) Merciful heaven! I see it all! Foul villain! this is your hellish work! Help! Help! (*Cries aloud.*)

SIR REG. (*Advancing stealthily towards her, with a fiendish smile.*) Be reasonable, sweet angel! Be reasonable. It is all over with you!

I have found you here, and that's all I know about it! You may
cease your cries! This is the rear of the house!

ALICE. (*With frenzied vehemence*) Miserable dastard! Is this the
means you have taken to gratify your grovelling spirit of revenge?
Whatever my fate, swift retribution will overtake you, and consign you
to the felon's doom you deserve! Disgraceful monster! (*With ineffable
scorn and disgust.*)

SIR REG. (*Dropping all disguise and bounding towards her.*) By
heaven! your doom is sealed, whatever may be mine!

(*At the same moment, ALICE, catching a glimpse of the handle of the
dagger, snatches the weapon from the book and brandishes it above
her head just as SIR REGINALD is about to lay hold of her.*)

ALICE. (*Fiercely.*) Back! dog! or I'll strike you dead at my feet!

(*SIR REGINALD recoils from the threatened blow, astounded. Before
he recovers himself, ALICE darts to one of the windows, breaks a
pane of glass with the handle of the dagger, and cries anew for help.*)

SIR REGINALD. (*Looking hastily about, as if in search of some weapon.*)
By heaven! I must put an end to this! What a fury! They'll hear
her in the alley! Curse that dagger! What noise is that? (*Hears
voices and hurrying footsteps on the stairs.*) By the God above me I am
foiled! I must fly! (*Springs for the secret door; but before he reaches
it TRAVERS, LESTER, and the DOCTOR burst into the apartment. The
two latter dash forward to seize him, but, having only got a glimpse of his
back, he disappears through the wainscot without being recognized by
them. In the meantime TRAVERS, with extended arms, rushes towards
ALICE, who totters towards him.*)

TRAVERS. (*Frantically.*) Alice! Alice! we but this moment learned,
at the solicitors', the character of this house!

ALICE. (*Dropping the dagger, and while falling insensible into his
arms.*) I am saved!

(*LESTER and the Doctor advancing towards TRAVERS, who stands
supporting ALICE in his arms, bending over her.*)

LESTER. (*In a state of great excitement.*) He has escaped, whoever
he may be!

DOCTOR. (*Bewildered and agitated.*) Yes! Through that secret door!
But I think I've seen that figure more than once ere this!

END OF ACT IV.

ACT V.

SCENE I.—*Servants' room in the Hermitage.* DICK WHITING, *with a perplexed expression of countenance, standing with one hand in his trousers' pocket, and leaning on a table with the other.*

DICK. There's summat up! Master away at daybreak this mornin', with Mr. Lester, as must have come back some time durin' the night! There's summat up! Ay, and more than summat! For Giles Goodwin told me but now, as how he met Gypsy Meg and Sarah Waters in the city lately, in Clifford street. There's summat up! That there be!

Enter SUSAN.

SUSAN. What's the matter Dick? The old housekeeper says you have been talking away to yourself for the last ten minutes.

DICK. (*Brightening up.*) Well, Susy dear, I was just thinkin' there's summat up; for the master has started off in a hurry with Mr. Lester to Lunnon, where Miss Alice, sweet creetur, is, as well as the Doctor and Master Travers, and where Giles Goodwin, as has just told me, met Gypsy Meg and Sarah Waters one arternoon, a few days since.

SUSY. That does look strange, Dick; and I hope nothing has happened to my dear mistress, that I have been crying my eyes out about! But I know there hasn't; for I heard Mr. Lester telling master in the hall, just as they were starting, that they'd all be back the day after to-morrow, to attend the fête the day following, when Sir Reginald comes into his estates, although, if I was Miss Alice, I wouldn't go a step!

DICK. I know, Susy; but then, you see, everybody is a goin' to hear what Mr. Lester says, and out of friendship for him only. And besides, I think most on 'em want to listen to the terrible ratin' he is goin' to give Sir Reginald afore he puts'n in possession of the papers.

SUSY. What are you going to do, Dick, when we all leave the Hermitage?

DICK. (*Lovingly and manfully.*) Susy, I be young, and have a stout arm, a clear conscience, and a heart as loves you bravely! I have, besides, sweet dear! eighteen pound five shillin's, without a dirty sixpence in it, as I have saved up for both on us; and what more does any one want to begin the world on?

SUSY. (*With hesitation.*) Dick, I wonder you think so much of me who worries and plagues you so!

DICK. (*With sudden energy.*) Think so much on you! Look here, Susy! (*Thrusting his hand into his bosom and drawing some things from it, which he places on the table before her.*) Them's what I wear next my heart!

Susy. (*Taking the articles up in the order in which she names them, and viewing each with surprise and emotion.*) Good gracious! One of my old gloves that I missed nearly a year ago! (*turning to the audience*)—a bit of cherry ribbon that I thought I lost in the wood last summer!—one of my side-combs! and half a dozen of my hair-pins tied together! Ah! Dick. (*Tenderly.*) Such love as this overpowers me! I feel I am scarcely worthy of it, and that it is now my time to ask you. (*Opening her arms and extending them towards him.*) Will you, Dick? (*Dick bounds forward, and they embrace affectionately.*)

Dick. (*Joyously.*) Susy, you have made a man on me! I am as strong as a giant!

Susy. (*Archly.*) Well, if you are, Dick, come and take down that Columbus for me, for I am going to dust the room, and fear that I should find it heavier then ever this morning.

Dick. Dear Susy, I'm ready to take'n down if he was a ton weight!

[*Exeunt.*

Scene II.—*At the door of the White Hart.* Mike *and* Capon *in deep conversation ;* Mike *gesticulating excitedly.*

Mike. Blur alive! And it's marr'ed you say they are, Misther Capon!

Capon. Ay; sure Mike! Marr'ed! She's Mistress Travers this mornin'! So Dick has told me. Bless her sweet soul!

Mike. Be the powers of pewther! I'm glad of it! Now, the joker at the Grange will have to mind his P's and Q's or else get his jacket dusted, besides bein' cut clear and clane out! But wasn't it very suddent?

Capon. It was main sudden; but, you see, Miss Alice was betrayed into some place in the city as wasn't right; and thinkin' that her good name might suffer by it, she was breakin' her heart, when Mr. Travers, to show what he thought on't, would marry her on the spot. So Mr. Mortimer was come for post-haste, and gid her away in presence of her aunt, the two solicitors and the Doctor and Mr. Lester, who comed for'n. But they don't want it spread for a day or two, for Mr. Travers still keeps on at the Grange. But I knew summat wonderful had taken place, because Miss Alice didn't take the governess situation, and I never seed her father so cheery for years! Mike, if I beant mistakin there's been queer goin's on in Lunnon within the last week or so, for I heerd privately, not an hour agone, as Gypsy Meg and Sarah Waters were seed there lately: ay! lad, and comin' out of the solicitors', too, with the Doctor and Mr. Lester! Isn't it surprisin'?

MIKE. Is that all you call it ? Surprisin' ! Why there's nothin' in the Irish Rogues and Rapparies to aquel it ! .

CAPON. Susy told me as she heerd Master Travers, when he comed home, swearin' vengeance against'n, and that, near as it was to his birthday, he'd gid'n a horsewhippin', and may be get a warrant again'n besides, for summat he did ; although I hear the Doctor and Mr. Lester begs on him to do nothin' to'n until the féte ; which makes me think that, may be, if he has done anythin' serious, they may have a warrant to clap on'n before all the people, with a good trouncin' at its back ! But, whether they clap a warrant on'n or not, no good can come on'n in the end ; for, as I often said, he's a bad'n as ever water wet !

MIKE. Oh ! then, sure no one of common sinse ought to attimpt to keep back the batin', whatever they might do wid the warrant ; that wouldn't spile for a day or two ; for, sure you know as well as I do that a batin' gets stale if it's kept a single hour, not to spake of a couple of days ! But I must go in and get my snares ready ; for Dick promised to help me to set them in the wood to-night.

CAPON. Mike, take my advice and have nothin' more to do with them snares of your'n now ; for, recollect, if Sir Reginald gets you into his clutches you won't get out on 'em so easy.

MIKE. Masther, dear, if I was to swing for it, I'll give them one thrial more, and that will be this very night, wid the help of the Lord and my own exarshuns. But, here's the Docther.   [*Exit* MIKE.

Enter DOCTOR HARLEY.

DOCTOR. Well, Ned, I suppose you've heard the news from Whiting or some of them ! If you have, you must keep it close till to-morrow afternoon. I have just called to tell you to bring some of the neighbors with you to the féte to-morrow ; for, after all, the people appear unwilling to turn out.

CAPON. So I have heerd, Doctor, I may get some on 'em to go ; but I know they don't like it ; he has been such a precious bad un !

DOCTOR. Well ! well ! Ned, we all know that ! But it is not out of compliment to him, you know, but to Mr. Lester, whom we all like ; and, besides, among some other few gentry, the young bride and bridegroom are going, to listen to the drubbing he'll get when Mr. Lester begins to speak, whom I am now just on my way to call upon.

CAPON. Doctor, its wonderful altogether ! Only think on't, Miss Alice and Master Travers man and wife !

DOCTOR. It's true, Ned, I was by when the knot was tied. But I must now be off ! Don't fail us to-morrow about eleven.
                                                        [*Exit* DOCTOR.

CAPON. (*Admiringly looking after the* DOCTOR.) Ay, he's a good'n !

But I must now go in and see what they are doin' ; for the nearer I get to leavin' these dear old walls, the more precious they grow in my eyes.

(*Enters the inn.*)

SCENE III.—*The wood, at dusk. Enter* DICK *and* MIKE, *approaching each other from opposite points ;* MIKE *with some rabbit-snares and strong whipcord across his arm.*

DICK. Here I be, Mike! (*They shake hands.*) Be you one on 'em as is swored in ?

MIKE. Of coorse I am, ma bouchal! and it's a magisthrate they'll make me yet, instead of a speshul constable, like you are now yourself, to help the two rale ones from the village keep the pace to-morrow, at the gatherin' over at the Manor; although the divil resaive the bit of me was ever able to keep it very well on me own account, lettin' alone that of others.

DICK. Yes, they be afeard that this great heir might get down some raggamuffins from Lunnon to hiss Mr. Lester; although it would be rather a ticklish job to hiss'n about these parts! Sir Reginald, I heerd, has been in the Manor a good bit of the day, a gettin' off that great speech of his'n, and throwin' his arms about like a windmill.

MIKE. Oh! dear! I suppose he'll bate Billy Pitt out and out! But, afther all, Dick, let me tell you that one of these got-off speeches, like a parrot, has no more strinth or heart in it than an ounce of bohay afther the third dhrawin'!

DICK. Are there many swored in besides us, for I haven't heerd ?

MIKE. 'Faix I b'leeve there is ; but the joker at the Manor doesn't know a word of it, for no one about here would tell him or Tony anythin'—the cutthroats! (*Suddenly seizes* DICK *by the arm and points towards something in the distance.*) See! Isn't that the long cloak and red hankercher of Gypsy Meg among the threes yondher ?

DICK. That it be, sure, Mike! I wonder what she's prowlin' about here now for ?

MIKE. Nothin' good, I'll warrant you! She's comin' this way ; let us slip behind this three, and take off our shoes. We'll make less noise when we're settin' the snares!

DICK. No, she beant; she has disappeared again; but as you say, let's take off our shoes and leave them at the root of this tree until we return. (*They take off their shoes, and listen from behind the tree for a moment.*)

MIKE. Softly! Dick, there's some one comin' up the path on the other side! Let us lie down! Maybe its the gamekeeper!

DICK. (*Peering through the twilight.*) No, it beant! I see'n! It's Master Travers comin' from the Hermitage and goin to the Grange.

Don't you hear'n hummin' a tune? Let us be still. I don't want'n to see us here at this hour!

MIKE. Yis, I hear him now. He's happy, Dick; and what often brakes my heart is, that I didn't finish that fella that took the Limerick girl from me, and ind my days airly like a good minny of my frinds and family!

(TRAVERS *now reaches the point where they stand concealed. When close beside them, still humming, unconscious of danger, a figure in a long gray cloak and red headdress glides stealthily from among the trees behind him, and steals noiselessly after him, with a long knife raised as if ready to strike.* DICK *and* MIKE *bound forward, and are just in time to arrest the murderous stroke; but not before a slight flesh-wound is inflicted upon* TRAVERS, *who turns suddenly round, and in the surprise and confusion of the moment, believing himself to be assailed by three assassins, cries,* "Help! Murder!" *while* DICK *and* MIKE *seize and overpower the intending assassin and possess themselves of the knife.*

MIKE. Don't be alarmed, Misther Thravers. It's Dick and Mike that's at your back! and that has just caught the arm of this she-divil as she was about to lave your noggin' and spoon idle! But we have nabbed her as nate and as clane as a whissel!—the gintle and tinder-hearted sowl!

DICK. Are ee hurt, Master Travers? Are ye hurt?

TRAVERS. (*Recognizing them both while they cling to the prisoner, who struggles to escape from them.*) Only a mere scratch, Whiting! Only a mere scratch, kind friends!

MIKE. Glad I'm of it, Misther Thravers! But hould this knife, if you plaze (*hands the knife*), for this sweet tulip of a gypsy—this bewtiful Meg, that I always knew was cut out for the gallis, is gettin' a little throublesome!

TRAVERS. Good friends, you are mistaken! Whoever this unfortunate wretch may be, rely upon it you have not made Gypsy Meg, as she is called, a prisoner! Examine her features and you will discover that I am correct!

MIKE. Oh! blessed hour! Did you ever hear the like of that? Why, look at her ould gray cloak and red handkercher, sir! Sure, there's no mistakin' her! But maybe, afther all, you're sayin' no more then the thruth!

DICK. I'll hold her, Mike, while you take a peep at her. (*Seizes the prisoner by the arms, and pinions them with his own.*)

MIKE. Come, young woman, as I hope you'll turn out to be durin' the operashun at laste, gi' me a kiss, till I see what kind of a mug you've got! (*Seizes the prisoner by the head, who struggles violently to prevent its being raised to expose the features.*) By the powers of pewther! young or ould, you are no joke any way, to puzzle Mike O'Grady in that style! But I'd have you know, ma'am, that I came from a counthry that never was bet on a kiss any way, no matther in what other respects it may have failed. (*Again struggles and succeeds in revealing the prisoner's face, into which he peers earnestly for a moment in the dim twilight. Suddenly.*) Oh! be the holy St. Dinnis! Oh! Misther Thravers! Hould on to him, Dick! Hould on to him! Be the ghost of a piper! it's Tony Lightfoot!

TRAVERS. I am not at all surprised. I suspected it was some infamous agent of that dastardly criminal whose career is about terminated.

DICK. Well, dash my buttons! if you beant in for it this time, Master Lightfoot! Let's bind'n with the snares and whipcord, Mike, before we take'n to the White Hart, where he'll be safe enough till he's under bolts and bars in the village!

MIKE. Sartinly, Dick! as a timperary officer of jistice I'll help you to spanshel, me boy, and slip a snare over his head too, that I can dhraw at leisure if he attimpts to cut up any capers! (*They bind him firmly, while he struggles violently to get out of their clutches.*)

TRAVERS. As he now seems perfectly secured, my friends, let us move towards the White Hart, where I shall look to this scratch of mine, while some one proceeds for Mr. Lester, who is the only magistrate close at hand.

TONY. (*Finding escape now impossible.*) I'll confess all, Mr. Travers, if you let me go!

TRAVERS. A full confession may lighten your punishment—may save your life! but it will never restore you to liberty!

TONY. Then I shall reveal all, this very night; and if I swing, my dear, kind, good master, who got me in this scrape, and others quite as bad, shall swing with me!

TRAVERS. Are you ready, friends?

MIKE. In rale marchin' ordher, sir! Dick, the shoes!

DICK. Yes, Mr. Travers, we be ready. (*Gets the shoes, etc.*)

TRAVERS. Then, let us move.   [*Exeunt.*

SCENE IV.—*Apartment in the Manor. Enter* SIR REGINALD *in a state of intense excitement.*

SIR REG. (*Pacing up and down.*) Fiends and furies! This is dangerous! Lightfoot in jail on a charge of attempt to murder! Curse the idiot, and his bit of a flesh-wound! Why didn't he send the knife home, as in the case of——(*Pauses.*) Well, it will all come right! He will keep his mouth shut; for he knows that I alone can help him now, and that, before the day closes, I shall be possessed of wealth enough to force his prison doors, if necessary, and set him at liberty! But should he peach! Good God! I must shut out that idea, and look to my coming triumph! There has been plotting against me! Lester and that Harley have been riding among some of my principal tenants, and, no doubt, prejudicing them against me regarding that Alice case; while this infernal affair will, of course, be laid pretty near my door by them also! I observe, in addition, that, within the last day or two, some strange influence has been working against me in the village, as many of the inhabitants who were previously polite at least, now turn their heads away when they see me. Ay, and even that Waters, whom, old as she is, I shall bundle out bag and baggage this afternoon with the rest of them, avoids me altogether of late! But what care I for any of them? The hour of my triumph is at hand, when I shall crush every one of them! I wish my messenger had been allowed to see Lightfoot this morning; but no matter. He knows on what side his bread is buttered! In the meantime I shall crush them one and all! Every soul under this roof shall be turned out of doors! The Mortimers shall be sent adrift without a shilling in their pocket, or even a hut that they can call their own to shelter them, while they can do nothing in that London affair, as I simply happened to drop in on Miss Alice in one of her haunts, for all I was to know! That fellow, Capon, goes too. Yes, goes—goes with the rest of them! But Lester is sole master here until noon, when, I learn, he will call upon me to come forward and relieve him of his trust. Five minutes after the hour, ay, one second, his power ceases; and I shall be close at hand to cut him short in whatever observations he may be making for the edification of his special friends who are to assemble at eleven. But I must now away and take another glance at that speech I have to make; for the hour draws near! But, fiends and furies! Lightfoot! Lightfoot!

[*Exit.*

SCENE V.—*In front of the White Hart.* CAPON, DICK, MIKE, *and others in a state of joyous excitement.*

MIKE. (*Shaking hands with everybody.*) Oh! be the mortial! I'll go out of my siven sinses! Tony has tould everythin! Aye, and sworn to it! And, what's more, it's all found out to be thrue! The millaynium is comin'! The millaynium his comin'! Hurroo! Hurroosh! (*Sings.*)

SONG.

One evenin', for divarshun sake, as I roamed out a-ga-lone,
I harde a-ga faymale lady bright o-ga! makin' her pittish moan.
She wrung her hair and tore her hands, and to herself did cry,
O-ga! Jonny-ga jewel don't murther me or else I'll surely-ga die!
(*Turning to* DICK.)

Fella me that in John's Lane, yer sowl ya! There's music for you, or I'm no botanist! Oh! Dick, alannah! (*Extending his hand*) lave it here. (*They shake hands.*) I'm in sich humor, that I could almost lay you dead at me feet!

DICK. (*While* CAPON *and others gesticulate in the background.*) Mike, I be almost crazy! Beant it a mericle?

3

MIKE. A mericle is it, you say! A mericle's only a child to it! He
has done enough to hang, thransport, dhraw and quarther him, and is
sure to spind the night wid Tony; for Misther Lesther sez there's a
whole ridgmint of warrants aginst him, although he doesn't suspect a
haporth about it, and will only be let into the saycret whin the darbies
are slipped on him by the two constables! And besides, his London
bewty is in jail by this time, too!

DICK. Ay, sure, and the whole on us, includin' Mr. Travers and his
sweet wife, will all be there to hear Mr. Lester gid it to'n afore he is
arrested. But then, Mike, he'll be so rich now that he'll be able to buy
hisself off, no matter what he does!

MIKE. I know, avick, that money can do a good dale; but its purty
hard to rub out blood wid anythin', as I know well; for whin a boy of
the Cumminses, in the County Tipperary, now minny a year ago, offered
thirty shillin's to a widda of the name of Mahar, for the murther of her
son Tady, she threw it in his face, and tould him to keep it, if that was
all he could do!

DICK. I suppose Master Capon has told ee that Suky and me is a
goin' under the one name purty soon.

MIKE. (With an air of melancholy.) Yis, Dick, he tould me all about
it. But I never like to spake of sich things now, bekase it brings back
that Limerick girl to me, and the blaggard that bamboozled me out of
her; may bad luck to him every day he sees a pavin' stone!

    (CAPON advances to MIKE and DICK, while the others walk and con-
      verse in the background, sotto voce.)

CAPON. (To DICK and MIKE.) I always said summat bad would come
on him. But it's hard to say what he may now manage with a goolden
key and lever, lads. And now if he's hanged, which he won't be, I'm
sartin, all his fine estates will go to the King, as there beant one in the
world as can claim em, so far as I knows on.

MIKE. Oh! then, the divil may care about the estates, so long as
he's laid out in lavendher. But sure we needn't throuble ourselves about
that; for I always knew that the day he died there would be a man
hung!

DICK. I suspect he'll be for cutting up a main purty caper when
they're puttin' the handcuffs on'n. But not a man, wooman, or child in
the village or on the estates but will be glad to get rid on'n, he has
been such a cruel bad un!

MIKE. Well, it's an ill wind that blows nobody good; for there will
be the greatest atin' and dhrinkin' over there that ever was seen in the
world, wid which he won't be able to intherfare; and I'll tell yez both
what, that so rejoiced am I wid the way he'll be hobbled, that I'll be
carr'ed home this blessed night, although the likes hasn't happened to me
since I once took a consolashun thrip to Ballinasloe Fair, whin I lost that
Limerick girl, whose sweet face, afther all, is wid me yet whin my eyes
are shut! Ah! Dick, mavourneen, and you Misther Capon, yez may say

what yez like, but whin the heart of a poor boy gets a kick, wid manin' in it, from the fut of the girl he loves, it's never the same shape aftherwards.

FROM THOSE IN THE BACKGROUND. Three cheers for Master Capon. (*They cheer,* DICK *and* MIKE *joining.*)

CAPON. (*Moved and gratified.*) Thank ee, lads and lasses! Thank ee from my heart! For I suppose it will be a long day afore you and me meet at the White Hart again; although, arter all, I beant out on it yet!

DICK. Ay, and three cheers for **Mr. Mortimer, Miss Alice, Mr. Travers,** and the Doctor. (*All cheer.*)

MIKE. Yis, begorra! and three cheers for Gypsy Meg, that seems to be betther stuff than any of us took her to be, afther all! (*They cheer again.*)

CAPON. Now, lads, it's not far from eleven o'clock; so let us make the best of our way to the Manor, and see the end of this main curious business. Come, lads and lasses. Come, along! It's close by.

[*Exeunt.* MIKE *capering off the stage.*

SCENE VI.—*The Manor. The hall door open.* LESTER, *with papers in his hand, addressing from the steps a number of excited villagers and tenants on the lawn. Ladies and gentlemen each side of him on the balcony, where* MORTIMER, ALICE, *in a highly nervous state,* TRAVERS *and the* DOCTOR *stand in a group, listening attentively. At the bottom of the steps, an officer of justice on either side, watching his movements intently. Enter* MEG, CAPON, MIKE, DICK *and* SUSAN, *conversing now and then in whispers.* MIKE *moves here and there occasionally, gesticulating when there's a pause.*

LESTER. Yes, my friends, as I **have** just said, this child, whom we all supposed so long dead, lives! but lives a scoundrel! a felon! under an assumed name! The gigantic crime to which he had, when two **years** old, been set as a seal, would have been brought to light long ago, **had** not one of the persons cognizant of it—Gypsy Meg, or rather Nancy Evans, who stands there disguised among you (*pointing to* NANCY, *who has just shaken hands with* CAPON)—been suddenly seized, at the time of its occurrence, as an English spy, and buried for years in the depths of a French prison, from which she has been but recently set free. Sarah Waters—the other person aware of this hellish plot—deposes she also would have revealed it long ago, had she not believed that a murder had been committed in connection with it, which was calculated to jeopardize her own safety. When, however, it was demonstrated lately to her by Nancy Evans, that, through her intervention, no blood had been spilled, she disclosed the whole affair; corroborating every syllable uttered by **Nancy,** whom some of you will

remember as the foster-sister of the late Lady Howard, and substan-
tiating, as does the sworn deposition of Nancy also, the dying disclosure
of a gentleman of the highest character and respectability, who, not
long since, departed this life a short distance from the city ; so that the
identity and history of this person, and, I may add, his crimes also,
have now been established before the proper authorities, beyond a
shadow of doubt !

   (*Here the clock in the turret strikes the hour of noon.   On the sound
   of the last stroke,* SIR REGINALD, *with a vicious leer of triumph,
   appears in the door-way, but without receiving the slightest recogni-
   tion from those on the balcony beside him, or from any one present.
   Stung by the terrible slight, a fierce scowl settles on his brow, and he
   disposes himself to listen for a moment to the thread of* LESTER's
   *remarks, who has paused, but who continues after the clock has
   ceased.*)

But, kind friends, the hour I perceive has now arrived when it becomes my duty to call upon Sir Reginald Howard to come forward and
relieve me of what you all know to have been a most painful trust. Before doing so, however, I shall make a few observations relative to the
manner in which I have been annoyed and embarrassed in the discharge
my onerous duties.

   (*At this point* SIR REGINALD *steps forward, cutting* LESTER *short.*)

   SIR REG. (*Superciliously and authoritatively.*) I believe, sir, I am now,
at last, lord and master here ! Hand me those papers ! (*Extending his
hand.*) We shall dispense with your explanations, as we shall with your
company, as well as with that of your particular friends also ! The
papers ! (*Great commotion and covert hissing and hooting on the lawn.*)

   LESTER. (*Eyeing him for a moment, and thrusting him back a step,
coolly.*) Don't anticipate ! Allow me to continue for a few moments !

   SIR REG. (*Recovering himself, and returning to the charge furiously.*)
Them papers, I say ! Hand me them papers ! You shall have no opportunity of traducing my character on my own door-steps, or of prejudicing the minds of these people in your favor, until you have first
rendered an account of your somewhat suspicious stewardship to me !

   LESTER. (*Composedly.*) That can be rendered on the spot, and in
the presence of all assembled, so far as I now have to deal with you.

                     (*Increasing excitement on the lawn.*)

   SIR REG. (*Stepping closer, and with wild vehemence.*) Them papers !
(*Stretches out his hand again.*) Hand me them papers, I say !

   LESTER. (*Calm and collected.*) Well, then, as you are so very
anxious to clutch these documents, you shall have the full benefit of
them at once ! They are, as you will perceive, four in number (*counts
them*); but these two (*selecting them and motioning to the officers of justice, who ascend the steps to where he stands*) will be quite sufficient for
the present ! This one (*handing it to one of the officers*) is a warrant for the arrest of Frederick Mansfield, for conspiracy against the

life of Sir Reginald Howard, resulting in an assault with intent to kill! This (*presenting the other paper to the second officer*) has been granted against the same villain, for feloniously betraying into a certain—(*here* SIR REGINALD *again interrupts him violently, but with some symptoms of vague and increasing alarm.*)

SIR REG. (*Now stands beside him and the two officers.*) What's all this mummery about? No one has assaulted me! No one has attempted my life! although there are some who are bad enough to do it! Come, sir, no more of this! It is with Sir Reginald Howard you have to deal at the present moment, and not with this Frederick Mansfield, whoever he may be!

LESTER. In that you are mistaken, for I shall deal with the villain Mansfield, first, who, when a child, had been substituted, in France, by his vile mother, for the true heir to these estates, and who now stands before this assemblage in your abhorred and infamous person! (*Excitement in the balcony and the wildest commotion and demonstrations of joy on the lawn.* MIKE *shaking hands with every one about him, while, on a signal from* LESTER, *the two officers seize* MANSFIELD *and handcuff him, before he has recovered from his horror and surprise.*)

MANSFIELD. (*Suddenly realizing his situation, and struggling violently to extricate himself from the hands of the officers.*) A conspiracy! A conspiracy to deprive me of my lawful heritage. (LESTER *ascends to the balcony and whispers to the* DOCTOR.)

MIKE. (*Sympathizingly, in a humorous attitude.*) Ah! then, blur an turf! What are you raisin' sich ructions for, Misther Mansfield? Take it aisy, man! take it aisy! Sure, afther all, you were only changed at nurse!—a thing that happens nearly every day wid us over there in Ireland! (*Merriment and laughter.*)

MANSF. (*Again suddenly horror-stricken. Aside.*) Great God! "Mansfield!" "Mansfield!" This, then, is the secret with which Waters has so often threatened me; but which I had long believed to be a mere groundless and selfish ruse on her part, for the purpose of keeping her purse well filled! (*Is led up the steps by the officers to the doorway of the Manor, where, with an officer on each side of him, he stands once more, while* LESTER *descends the steps again, amid cheers and joyful exclamations.*)

LESTER. (*Restoring silence and order with a wave of his hand.*) There is neither conspiracy nor falsehood about it, my friends! You can all satisfy yourselves, both here or on application to the proper authorities in the city, that the person who has been just handcuffed in your presence as a felon—and who with his accomplice Tony Lightfoot, now in prison, has been guilty of offences the most criminal and heinous—has usurped or assumed the name and rank of the true heir to these estates for upwards of twenty years! whom the unprincipled mother of this wretch fancied she had consigned securely to an early and bloody grave. But, through the benign interposition of a merciful Providence, and the undying love and fidelity of his old nurse Nancy Evans, he lives, and stands on English soil to-day!—a fact established upon the broadest possible basis, and which can be substantiated, to a singular extent, by even your old friend, Dr. Harley himself. (*Turning to the* DOCTOR.)

(*Cheers, and cries of Long live the true* SIR REGINALD! *Long live* NANCY EVANS! *Upon which,* NANCY *divests herself of her red head-dress and long cloak, and, throwing them over* CAPON'S *arm, stands attired in a modest cap and plain dress. The* DOCTOR *advances in the meantime, and takes up a position a step or two above* LESTER, *a little on one side.*)

DOCTOR. Yes, my friends, it is true! My memory, and my diary, which I have posted regularly daily for the last thirty years, set forth that, on the same day, and when they were about seventeen or eighteen months old, I vaccinated two children. One was Reginald, the only child of the late Sir Arthur and Lady Howard—the other, the son of a Widow Mansfield, to whose guardianship young Howard was entrusted after her ladyship's death, Sir Arthur having died 'previously. I performed the operation, if I may so term it, on the upper part of the arm of the widow's son, whose name I have entered as Frederick; but, to gratify a whim of Lady Howard, who did not wish to have any mark in sight on the fair round limb of her little darling, I applied the infection to the under part of his arm, the cicatrice resulting from which I have recently found, in this latter place, on the person of the true Sir Reginald; while I have been enabled to ascertain that the mark resulting from vaccination is clearly visible on the upper part of the arm of the prisoner, although the under is totally free from any traces of the sort!

(MANSFIELD *with muttered imprecations still stands in the doorway glaring about him like a chained hyena, while the* DOCTOR *rejoins his party.*)

CAPON. (*Turning to* NANCY.) I always said he looked no more like Sir Arthur or my lady than I be; and, besides, I never could help thinkin' as summat bad would come on him.

NANCY. You are right, old friend! There is not even the most remote resemblance between that man and my poor, dear master or mistress, now long in the grave!

LESTER. But now, kind friends, as already intimated, the time has fully arrived when it becomes my duty to place these large estates in the possession of their rightful owner, and this I shall proceed to do with supreme pleasure, as he and his lovely and amiable young wife are standing amongst us at the present moment! But, before doing so, I shall avail myself of the high honor and profound gratification of presenting them to you personally! (*Cheers.*)

(*Ascends the steps and approaches the group, where the* DOCTOR *stands conversing with* MR. MORTIMER, ALICE, *and her husband. Some ladies and gentlemen throng around him, all speaking together, sotto voce; while* MANSFIELD *still stands listening and glaring about him ferociously; and cries of "Long live Mr. Lester!" "Long live the true Sir Reginald and Lady Howard," ascend from those below: MIKE being particularly lively and happy, with a handsome servant girl now hanging on his arm.)*

MIKE. (*Approaching* DICK, *who stands beside* SUSAN, *and giving him a slap on the shoulder.*) Dick! me hayro! The millaynium is come! the millaynium is come! Hurroo! Poor as I am this minnet, I'd give a hundhred pounds of me masther's money if I could only but turn a summerset like a showman! Be the mortial, the heart will fly out of me!

DICK. (*Eyeing* MIKE'S *conquest with a knowing smile.*) I think the millanium *be* come, Mike, and that the heart has flied out on you too: but not home to that Limerick lass you're always a talkin' about.

MIKE. (*Taken a little aback.*) Limerick lass! Arrah! what do you mane! (*Pauses in thought for an instant.*) Oh! sorra take you and your "lass," instead of "girl"—the one I refused, you mane? Well, she thried hard to get me; but d'ye see, my dear mother, the heavens be her bed, made me take a solemn oath to her, in her last moments, that I'd never marry out of the family, barrin' an English girl!

(CAPON *and* NANCY *join them.*)

CAPON. This is a wonderful day, lads and lasses! and Ned Capon has lived to see it; and beant out of the White Hart yet!

DICK. It is a wonderful day, Master Capon, and none on us at the Hermitage be in much danger of goin' out either, whoever the new Sir Reginald and lady may be!

SUSAN. I think you're right, Dick; and if you are, you'll have a few more opportunities of taking down that heavy Columbus off the mantel-piece for me!

NANCY. (*Smilingly.*) Yes, good friends; but I have just learned, that, in a day or two, you intend to begin taking it down in partnership.

MIKE. (*Turning to his coy acquaintance, lovingly.*) D'ye hear that, asthore! and the soft heart within me, like a lump of fresh butther waitin' for the prent!

LESTER *now takes* TRAVERS *and* ALICE *by the hand, standing between them, and, followed by* MORTIMER *and the* DOCTOR, *commences to descend from the balcony.* MANSFIELD, *perceiving how terrible this portion of his retribution, gives a fierce shriek, and is hurried by the two officers off the stage. The party from the balcony advance,* LESTER, ALICE, *and* TRAVERS *in front,* MORTIMER. *the* DOCTOR, *and* CAPON, *on the side of* ALICE, *and* NANCY, DICK, SUSAN, *and* MIKE, *who has relinquished his companion, on the side of* TRAVERS. NANCY *close to him. As they approach the foot-lights, the villagers and tenantry fall back on either side, with cheers and joyful cries, "It's Miss Alice!" "It's Mr. Travers!" "Long live Lady Mortimer Alice!" "Long live the noble Sir Reginald Travers!" and finally, "Long live the true Sir Reginald and Lady Howard!"*

LESTER. (*Looking towards the tenantry, etc., and turning then, and bowing to the audience with a face radiant with smiles.*) And, now, kind friends on all sides, I have the unspeakable happiness of presenting to you, in the person of the recent poor tutor at the Grange, the true heir to the estates of Gray Cliff Manor, which I now formally place in his possession (*handing him a sealed package*), and with him, his noble and beautiful young bride! Dear friends, Lady and Sir Reginald Howard! (*Immense cheering and excitement, while SIR REGINALD and ALICE bow to the villagers and audience, with great cordiality and radiant faces. LESTER and ALICE now retire a step to one side and enter, sotto voce, into conversation with CAPON, the DOCTOR, and MORTIMER; MIKE, DICK, SUSAN, and NANCY, on the side of SIR REGINALD, doing the same among themselves, NANCY within reach of SIR REGINALD. On the termination of the cheering, and just before SIR REGINALD, who keeps his position, speaks; MIKE leans slightly forward as if to get another view of him and LADY HOWARD.*)

MIKE. (*Throwing up his arms in the most blank amazement.*) Oh! Be all the saints in the red-letther calandher! Is it start, starin' mad I am, or can I b'leeve me eyes! (*Turning to DICK.*) Dick! That settles me! We're all changed at nurse!

SIR REG. (*On quiet being restored, turning alternately to all on the stage and the audience.*) Although for some time aware, kind friends, that my birth was involved in mystery, I little thought, until within the last few days, that I should stand before you on the present occasion, the acknowledged son and heir of the late Sir Arthur and Lady Howard. For this I am to thank a protecting Providence, and the undying love and fidelity of my mother's foster-sister, my old nurse, Nancy Evans (*turns to NANCY and kisses her in the forehead*), who, the day before she had been thrown into prison, had obtained the name and address of a Reverend Gentleman into whose care I had been accidentally thrown, and who proved a kind father to me. On her release from her long years of captivity, she, still true to her love and her vows, took up this clue, and traced me to this place, to which she naturally gravitated, and to which I had been led by a benign and mysterious power! But, as the dear friend of my father, and the faithful guardian of these estates (*turning to LESTER and shaking hands with him*), apprised me this morning, that my more intimate acquaintance with you would be best commenced and explanations made at a banquet prepared for us both on the lawn and in the Manor, we shall, with the kind permission of those (*bowing to the audience*), without whose sanction the viands would be unsavory indeed, now retire, and close, in the midst of good fellowship and good cheer, this long comedy, in which all of us appear to have played some part, and which had been so NEARLY A TRAGEDY. (*Immense cheering and demonstrations of joy.*)

TABLEAU.

Sir Reg. and Lady H.
 Nancy,   Mort.,
  Sus.,   Doc.,
 Dick,   Lester,
Mike,   Cap.

CURTAIN FALLS.

THE END.